Faye & The Music Fairies

Crescendo

Paul Govier-Simpson

Text Copyright ©2015 Lyssa-Jade Woolley (Nee Simpson)
The right of Paul Govier-Simpson to be identified as the author of this work has been asserted by her daughter, Lyssa-Jade Woolley.
All rights reserved.
ISBN:9798327245624

This book is sold subject to the condition that it shall not, by way of trade or otherwise, be lent, hired out or otherwise circulated in any form of binding or cover other than that in which it is published.
No part of this publication may be reproduced, stored in a retrieval system, transmitted in any form of means (electronic, mechanical, photocopying, recording or otherwise) without the written permission of Lyssa-Jade Woolley, Copyright holder.

Illustrations Copyright ©2021 Joelle Henry

OTHER BOOKS IN THE FAYE & THE MUSIC FAIRIES SERIES

1 The Clef Crystal

2 Scales

3 Dee Sharp

4 Woodwind

5 Crescendo

6 Tutti

ACKNOWLEDGEMENTS

A huge thank you to everyone who has patiently waited for book 5 to be released - my (now) husband and I have had an incredibly tough year this past year (2023/2024) and so unfortunately the final two books have been the last things on my mind until now.

As always a massive thank you to the wonderful Hannah for doing the proof reading - it gets harder each book i'm sure!

Finally, I would not have these books finished without the amazing Jo, my wonderful designer, who's covers are just stunning and make these books complete. Thank you for all your hard work, and for sticking with me these past 3 years!

A Note From The Authors Daughter

I honestly did not realise what an undertaking these books would actually be to get published - I thought it would take me a couple of months max to get them all typed, proofread and ready for designs to be made, before releasing them to the world. Oh how WRONG I was!
Instead, here we are in May 2024, just releasing book 5 - 3 years after launching book 1, 2 & 3, and 2 years since launching book 4!

A lot has happened in the last 2 years to force my hand in putting these books on the back shelf, waiting for the right time to get the last 2 out there, and I'm so pleased that soon all 6 books will be complete, and I will have fulfilled my promise to Mum.

Mum - as always, this is for you.
Love you always my butterfly Fairy.

Lyssa -x-

CHAPTER 1

The mist swirled this way and that; looking for a way inside, a way to work its evil magic on the occupants of the room it could not reach.

Suddenly, it was roughly thrust aside by beating wings and figures, with glass orbs over their heads and a box-like creation strapped to their backs.

As they reached the door the larger figure turned and vigorously waved a huge leaf fan, which wafted the mist away from the door.

At the same time, the smaller figure heaved the door open just wide enough for both of them to enter, then the door was shut tight against the pernicious Woodwind once more!

As Rollo removed his helmet, he was concerned to see Landler kneeling beside Polka, who was coughing heavily.

"Landler! Polka! Are you alright?"

Landler, who had been lost in concern for his mate, started violently as he looked up.

"Rollo! Help me - she can't stop coughing!"

Presto, having put down the box he was carrying, had already fetched a glass of water and knelt down the other side of Polka.

"Here, drink this."

She took the glass gratefully and sipped.

Rollo took the out bottle of Vivace Drops he always carried in his pouch and gave the gasping Fairy three drops. Almost at once, Polka stopped coughing.

"Thank you, Rollo," she gasped, wiping her streaming eyes with a handkerchief.

Landler got up. "Vivace Drops! Why didn't I think of that?

Polka brought some with her! Stupid!" He berated himself, crossing to the window looking out.

"You were too busy getting us to safety," Polka replied, loyally. (She had walked out to meet him and got caught in the first wave of the Woodwind.) "I'm better now."

"<u>Us</u>?" queried Presto - then noticed, for the first time, the curious cluster of animals dotted around the room.

Three adult deer (one Stag and two Doe's), plus their fawns were grouped over on the far side. An assortment of rabbits, squirrels and mice huddled together under an old table in the corner; <u>all</u> of them were keeping a wary eye on the third group, which consisted of a family of foxes, two stoats and four ferrets who were maintaining an uneasy alliance in the face of a common danger, whilst five owls flew around the room in agitation.

"Did you bring them all in <u>with</u> you?" asked Presto, amazed.

"Well, I carried a few... some already had a head start on us and gave the warning that something was coming... and the rest followed."

"What are we going to do with them?" Presto queried. "We can't take them all with us!"

Rollo looked around at all the animals, then nodded to himself.

"Presto, can you get them all into the barn round the back?"

"<u>In</u> <u>this</u>?" Presto pointed outside.

"There is an underground tunnel, leading from the pantry; use that." (A feature that Monody's Great Grandfather has insisted on having built, as he had the greatest dislike of storms, and wanted a way in which he could reach his animals and calm them, without getting soaked!)

As Presto picked up the smaller animals, Rollo said quietly in his ear, "Put the predators of the third group into the stone-room in the barn. I'm going to get food for them, but if it runs out before we can return and free them, best not leave them with a live food-source!"

"Good point!" murmured Presto.

By the time Rollo had found the Maestro's supply of animal food, (he liked to go into the forests and tempt the fawns and squirrels to eat from his hands) and taken some particularly fine-looking joints of meat from the cold shelf in the pantry, Landler had helped Polka into the nearest chair, and she was looking a lot better.

Rollo, having made sure the animals had straw, food and plenty of water, glanced out of the window again as he returned.
"How are you feeling now, Polka? Do you think you're up to travelling?"
"Travelling? Landler frowned. "Where to?"
"The Red Barn," replied Presto, joining them. "It's the closest place of safety."
"What do you mean - safety?" Landler got up. "What's happening?!"
"We'll discuss it all once you're back at the Red Barn," Rollo replied firmly.
Polka glanced up and saw the worry in the usually calm Fairies face.
"I'm much better, thank you, Rollo. Let's go, shall we?"

In the next few minutes, Polka had been fitted with a mask and oxytank, as had Landler.
Rollo signaled that he was going to open the door and indicated that they should all hold hands.
As soon as they were outside, Landler understood why. The thick green mist swirled around them, making any sense of direction impossible.
Rollo, however, led them to the right, until he literally bumped into their transport waiting for them.
Rollo and Presto hoisted Polka onto the back of "Brand!"
Polka recognised Landler's Beamer friend at once and patted him. She felt Landler climb up behind her and was reassured when she felt his arms about her waist.
Rollo and Presto had disappeared, but when Polka felt along Brand's back, her fingers touched a harness, and then she knew: Rollo and Presto were behind them... on Brio, the

Beamer Butterfly who had saved Faye and lost an eye in the process.

He flew on a harness behind Brand, and, as they took off, Polka could only be thankful that the Music Fairies had such good allies that could be relied upon to risk their own lives to help their friends!

***

By the time the group arrived back at the Red Barn, it was clear that the Beamers had been affected by the Woodwind.

Rollo had, quite literally, thrown together two contraptions that he hoped would serve as some sort of protection for the butterflies, but it was now clear that, although they kept a lot of the mist out, some had seeped in and been inhaled.

As the Fairies climbed down from the saddles, first Brand, and then Brio had staggered slightly; both had lost their normal bright colours and were looking decidedly grey.

Rollo set up a yell for the Beamer Medics, and four of them suddenly appeared and led their two patients away.

Seeing Landler torn between going with Brand and wanting to make sure Polka was alright, Presto said, "Stay with Polka, Landler. I'll go and see what the medics say about Brand and Brio."

Landler cast his friend a grateful look.

"Thanks, Presto."

Rollo had gone in to organise things, and by the time Landler had taken Polka to see Viola, who would be able to give her something for that cough, which hadn't completely stopped, there was enough food and drink laid out on one of the many tables in the main hall, to satisfy a small army. People at the Red Barn had a habit of passing through when they were hungry and collecting food and drink on their way to the next task, rather than having a set time to eat, apart from the evening meal, which they took together when all had finished their work for the day.

Landler took Polka to a nearby table and sat her down, before going to fill plates for both of them, ignoring her comment of, "I can get my own food, Landler."

"You stay there - you're still coughing!"

She smiled at him.

"It's much better now, but I'll stay here if I must, dearest."

"You must," he smiled back at her.

Rollo came back to sit down just as Landler returned with a tray bearing four heaped plates, mugs and a jug.

"I brought food for everyone."

"Thanks, Landler. If I don't eat now, who knows when I'll get another chance!" Rollo snatched up a couple of rolls and a mug of Lupin tea.

"Well," began Landler, "before you get called away, can I first say thank you for coming to our rescue," here Polka nodded in agreement. "And secondly, <u>what</u> is going on?"

Rollo took a deep breath - he knew Landler well enough to know that he was about to become very angry.

He was right.

"You mean to tell me that the Maestro knew all about this... what did you call it... Woodwind? On the day of our Handclasping, and instead of telling me, he packs me off to his own personal villa to hide... like a coward?!"

Landler's voice had risen with every word, and as he slammed his fist on the table at the end of his rant, every Fairy in the hall looked round, startled.

Polka lay a gentle hand on his arm.

"Dearest, no one could <u>ever</u> accuse you of being a coward. I'm sure the Maestro had a very good reason to do what he did."

It was, perhaps, fortunate that Presto came back from the medic's wing at this moment. Landler immediately pounced on him.

"How's Brand? Is he alright?"

Presto nodded as he sat down.

"Yes, they're both okay, but they're very weak. It's as though the mist sapped their strength. They are going to need a lot of rest, before they undertake any more journeys." He looked at Landler with meaning.

"But I can't be stranded <u>here</u> - I need to get back to the Maestro - how can we stop this thing if we can't get together to formulate a plan?" He looked at each of them.

"Landler," Rollo gripped his shoulder, "<u>listen</u>, this is what we know so far. Forlana and the Maestro are running things at Cadence Falls; Fanfare and the Professors no doubt have everything under control at Scores Hall, and Faye and Peri have gone back to their own world to rest, although the Maestro did say they would be returning soon."

"I'll send a message to Cadence Falls, then." Landler started to rise, when Presto's next words halted him.

"No Landler, that won't work. The robins and fireflies can't survive the Woodwind - we know that for a fact!"

Landler sat down again and thought of his favourite little firefly who always came when he whistled - Landler hoped he was alright.

"You'd better tell me everything, Presto."

Rollo looked at his friend and nodded, so Presto relayed all that they knew; how there had been deaths in Galliard and Bagatelle, how no one knew in which direction the Woodwind would travel next, (they had proof of this in the fact that Pavane Villa lay in the opposite direction to Galliard and Bagatelle - the very reason the Maestro had sent them there, and yet the Woodwind had reached the villa, even though it had not got as far as the Red Barn… yet.)

In fact, if Monody had not sent out a final robin (who died shortly after it arrived) to tell Rollo he feared the Woodwind was already heading for Pavane Villa, Landler and Polka could well have been trapped there.

Finally, Landler sat staring at his hands for a moment, before saying, "Very well, if we can't contact the others, and we <u>can't</u> leave… Let's make ourselves useful <u>here</u>!" He turned to Rollo. "What can we do?"

Rollo heaved a sigh of relief.

"<u>Thank you</u>, Landler, Polka. What <u>I</u> need, more than anything, is someone to take charge! Presto and I are rushed off our feet, trying to make as many masks and oxytanks as we can. Once this Woodwind gets here - no one will be able to go outside without wearing them. We may need to gather more food and medicines - we <u>have</u> to have enough masks. Polka, I know of your skills with distilling herbs and plants - would you be willing to organise a team? We're going to need so much more than usual."

"Of course," Polka smiled, gently cutting across Landler as he was about to argue. "It's much better to keep busy while we're here, don't you agree, dearest?"

After looking at her for a moment, Landler sighed.

"Just don't do too much, Polka," he begged.

"I'll be fine, honestly. I just wish we knew that Forlana was alright."

Landler laughed. "Her? She'll be in her element - bossing people about - and she has the Maestro there to keep her in line!" he added as he saw Presto's comical expression; Forlana could be scary, sometimes!

As they started to clear things away, Landler voiced a concern that had occurred to him.

"Rollo, one thing I <u>would</u> like to organise, with your permission, is to put the storage rooms in order, so we know <u>what</u> we have."

"Why?" asked Presto. "Surely that can wait?"

Landler looked at him, seriously.

"When Rollo and I were looking for something - <u>anything</u> that would enable me to go into the Cacophony Wood when Faye was taken prisoner, we wasted <u>so</u> much time, rummaging about in stuff we <u>didn't</u> need. That was time that we didn't have. Faye nearly died as a result." His reminder made them all realise how important this was.

"If we find ourselves in a similar situation, it is vital we know <u>what</u> we have and <u>where</u> it is!"

Rollo nodded. "Of course, Landler. Pick whoever you need to help, but not Presto - I need him!"

"Fair enough," grinned Landler, getting to his feet.

Polka took the tray over to a small table near the kitchens.

"You choose whoever you need, too, Polka!" Rollo called after her.

"Thank you, I will."

The four friends then spent the rest of the day occupied with their own separate tasks, and if Polka looked a little pale and tired by the time they all sat down for the evening meal, it was only to be expected after the eventful day they'd had.

Viola popped in to tell Polka that she'd arranged a little room at the back of the hall, near the shell-baths which Faye had enjoyed so much on her first visit there.

"It's not very big," Viola apologised, but was cut short by Landler.

"If it's big enough to sleep in, we'll be happy."

Polka nodded in agreement, trying to stifle a yawn.

Viola laughed. "It's this way."

The friends said goodnight, each ready for a good night's sleep to prepare them for the events which were to come.

CHAPTER 2

Under a beautiful cherry-blossom tree, which stood on the little green just across the way from the Falls, sat a lone Fairy. She rested her head on her hand, as she gazed into the clear, sparkling water that fell into the pool below.

It was Forlana's favourite place to sit on a summer's evening, but now her head was swimming with so many thoughts that she couldn't enjoy it as she usually did.

It had been a long day and she'd spent most of it creating a distillery in Landler's old cottage with Fretta and Minima - two of the Music Fairies who had more talent with herbs and plants than she could ever possess! (The little knowledge she had, she'd learnt from Polka.)

As she thought of her best friend, Forlana angrily brushed a tear away. She couldn't bear crying - seeing it as a sign of weakness, besides, Polka did enough weeping for the whole of Cadence Falls!

However, not knowing if Polka and Landler were alright was worrying her so much that when she suddenly heard footsteps behind her, she jumped.

"I'm sorry, my dear. I didn't mean to startle you." The Maestro came round to stand in front of her. "I just came to see if you were alright."

"Sorry, Maestro, I was miles away - I'm fine, really."

Monody looked into her eyes, and didn't believe her. He sat down on an old, broken tree-stump. wishing for the hundredth time that there were some smooth rocks or boulders nearby that they could use as seats: wood had many splinters.

"You're worried about Landler and Polka."

He said it as a statement, not a question.

"If I just knew they'd got out safely!"

"I know, my dear. But remember, as soon as that message arrived from Scherzo, (a tiny village to the East) saying they'd spotted a strange green mist heading in a South-Easterly direction, I sent a robin to Rollo at the Red Barn, telling him to go and fetch them without delay - he will definitely have done so!"

"Yes - <u>if</u> the message reached him... but we don't know that it <u>did</u>!"

Monody frowned... the bird that had brought the message from Scherzo must have flown through the Woodwind, as it died shortly after the Maestro had seen <u>his</u> robin off on its journey to the Red Barn. The robin had not returned, so Monody could only hope that meant Rollo had kept it in, <u>not</u> that it had died before reaching its destination.

He reached out and took Forlana's hand.

"You know, better than <u>anyone</u>, how resourceful your brother is. He will find a way to keep Polka safe, at all costs!"

"Yes, he will" Forlana gave a little smile.

Her brother had fallen head over heels in love with her best friend - in fact they had only just celebrated their Handclasping a few days ago, but when the Maestro had heard of this strange, green 'Woodwind' - he'd packed them off to his own private home, in the hopes of keeping them safe... and now, it appeared, they weren't.

"We must continue to hope for the best, Forlana, although I must admit I have been doing my fair share of worrying, too." He sighed. "I don't know if this Woodwind has reached Scores Hall or not - I don't even know if Fanfare and the bluebirds made it back alright."

Forlana gasped - in her concern for Polka and her brother, she had forgotten about the fussy little herald. Despite his irritating manner, she knew he was invaluable to Monody, taking care of many of the day-to-day details of the running of Scores Hall; he also took care of all the magical creatures that lived there, and seemed to have a knack of knowing what his master needed almost before Monody himself did.

"I'm sorry, Maestro," Forlana apologised, "of course - you must be just as worried as I am!"

He nodded. "I wish I knew that all my people at Scores Hall were safe, but there's nothing i can do about it at present, so I take comfort in knowing that there are Fairies there who are more than capable of running things." (He meant, of course, the other members of the Circle of Five, but he couldn't mention that to Forlana - as it was a secret, known only to a few.)

Forlana nodded, then in her usual brisk manner said, "Talking of running things, the distillery is ready for use as soon as we get more supplies."

"Good! Crumhorn and Dash have done an excellent job of turning the Warehouse into a base of operations where we can meet every night. There is so much to organise that we'll require all the different groups to tell us what they've done, and what they need."

"I'll collect the lists from everyone and go through it all, putting what's needed in order of importance, then I'll give it to you."

"Where it will be my job to try and provide it." He smiled, ruefully.

"One thing I have done, Forlana, is to send all the barrels of discarded Dots from the Warehouse back to Scores Hall to be decontaminated."

(No one quite knew how this was done, and no-one was going to ask, but the fact was the Maestro used a very mild translocation spell, so that the barrels simply disappeared from the Warehouse, and reappeared at Scores Hall.)

"I don't know if the Woodwind could activate them," he continued, "but I'm not taking any chances on them escaping, and going into the Cacophony Wood, where Dee Sharp would lose no time turning them into Discords!"

Forlana shuddered. She'd heard Faye's account of what the Discords were like, and she certainly didn't want to risk having to deal with them as well as the Woodwind!

"Is it really coming here?" she asked Monody in a small voice.

"We have to assume so," he nodded.

"But, I don't understand how it can be in Bagatelle and Galliard, which lie to the West, then be spotted travelling towards Pavane Villa in the South-East?"

"I can't be sure, of course," replied Monody, slowly, "but it's my belief that in all the years she's been there, Dee Sharp never strays very far from the castle. It's the centre of her power, so it makes sense that she'd stay near it. Most of the villages around the Cacophony Wood have sprung up after she came to be there."

(Indeed, a few had sprung up because she was there!)

"I don't think she knows the layout of her surroundings. Remember, this Woodwind is travelling by magic - oh, it may occasionally get caught up in a breeze, but Dee Sharp will have set its course. I imagine she has sent it off in two or three directions in the hopes that, sooner or later, it will reach one of our villages… which, of course, it has." He paused, while they both thought of the Fairies and creatures that had died as a result.

"However," he went on more briskly, rising and helping her up, "I think two possibilities may occur, both to our advantage. The first is that, in order to <u>see</u> if her plan has worked, she may be forced to leave the castle and come to the Bar Barrier, and the second is that using all this dark magic will weaken her considerably. Put these two things together and we <u>may</u> have a chance to defeat her!"

"Do you really think we can, Maestro?"

"I have to believe so," Monody said firmly.

As he had been talking, he'd led her, almost without her realising it, back towards her cottage.

As they neared the door, Forlana said, "You go in, Maestro. I just want to pop into the treatment centre, (the name they had decided on for Landler's old cottage) and check everything is ready for tomorrow, when all the mattresses and bedding will start arriving."

"Very well, my dear. I'll see you in the morning." Monody went off to the guest room for a well-deserved rest.

Forlana, having said goodnight, turned and went, <u>not</u> next-door, but across the street to the new cottage that Landler had so lovingly prepared for his new soulmate.

She went from room to room, gazing around at the beauty and emptiness of it, then collapsed onto a chair and sobbed her heart out.

CHAPTER 3

He had to stop; he had to rest! His leg was burning as it never had before. He'd been walking all night long, unsure of his direction in the dark - only knowing he had to put as much distance as possible between himself and the evil enchantress he had come to despise.

Dirge collapsed near a dry, shrivelled bush that lurked next to a mis-shapen dead tree. Gasping with the pain in his leg, he reached for his water bottle and took a tiny sip, being very careful with it, for he had no idea how long it would take him to find water again; certainly not in this dark, dismal place.

He took the scrap of cloth from his pocket, wiped the top of the bottle and pushed the stopper back in before stowing it carefully back in his knapsack.

He looked at the torn material in his hand. The remains of what looked like a red poppy danced in the corner. He'd found it just as dawn was breaking. He'd nearly fallen over the odd-shaped mound that blocked his way. Bending down and clearing the dirt from it, he discovered it to be what looked like part of a saddle!

Dirge was puzzled. No animal could have wended its way through the wood, there wasn't room! Also, no Music Fairy could survive there - that much he <u>did</u> know, having witnessed two of them collapse and die, many moons ago.

This now saddened him in a way that it hadn't at the time.

He stared at the saddle again - not a Fairy, no... a dim recollection came to him. Dee Sharp had captured two little creatures - what were they called? He couldn't remember, but there was a bat, lying dead on the floor, when he was summoned, and... yes, someone else was there - who was it? Try as he might, Dirge couldn't quite recall... but it suddenly seemed important to him that he <u>should</u> remember.

He looked at the poppy-embroidered scrap once more, then put it in his pocket. Maybe, once he was safe, it would help him remember... <u>once</u> he was safe.

A sudden noise overhead sent him scuttling for cover. He knew what it was immediately - a Discord, sent to seek him out - that meant Dee Sharp knew he had deserted her!

Very carefully, Dirge drew in his injured leg, which he had stretched out in front of him, and, just as carefully, turned <u>under</u> the bush, so he was hidden from view.

Hardly daring to breathe, he waited.

The Discord zipped this way and that, searching, hovering, till, eventually, he heard it moving away. Fighting the instinct to break cover and get away as quickly as possible, Dirge stayed where he was.

Sure enough a little while later, the Discord was back, in exactly the same place, waiting, as if taunting him, daring him to come out.

It took every ounce of self-control <u>not</u> to move. His injured leg was now becoming cramped, but he knew if he moved and the Discord spotted him it would mean instant death, so Dirge bit his lip against the pain and, after what seemed like forever, was rewarded with the unmistakable sound of the Discord speeding up and returning to the castle.

Waiting another five minutes, just to be sure, Dirge stretched out his leg, clapping his hand over his mouth, as a groan of agony escaped his lips. He lay there panting for a while, intending to go on as soon as the pain became bearable again, but when he tried to get to his feet, he soon discovered he couldn't stand, let alone walk!

Sobbing with terror, he tried to think of a plan. He had no idea how far or near the edge of the wood lay, nor what he would find when he came out of it. The Music Fairies certainly wouldn't be prepared to help <u>anything</u> that came out of the Cacophony Wood. The only thing he could think of was to try and find a hiding place near a stream, (he <u>had</u> to have a supply of fresh water!) and recover his strength to the point where he could continue his journey to get as far away from Dee Sharp as possible.

Dirge had already decided that one of the first things he <u>must</u> do was to warn the Music Fairies about the green mist, (even though they might attack him on sight and probably wouldn't believe a word he said!)

He couldn't explain <u>why</u> he suddenly felt it was so important to save the Fairies, but he knew it was!

Exhausted by his travels and all these new emotions, it was little wonder that Dirge now fell asleep, where he was.

When he startled awake, several hours later, he sat up in panic.

It was dark! How long had he been asleep? Suppose Dee Sharp had set off after him the second the Discord had got back? She'd be hard on his heels now - he'd never get away!

Then a thought occurred to him. She wouldn't know which way he'd gone, because <u>he</u> didn't know which way he'd gone! The Discord <u>hadn't</u> found him!

Taking several deep breaths to steady himself, Dirge put some weight on his bad leg - true, it hurt, but not with the agony he had endured, earlier, (the rest had done it good!)

He stood up and stretched, cautiously... He could hobble along on it, much as he used to do before he strengthened it, going up and down the castle steps to the dungeons, to play his beloved oboe which he'd found there.

The trouble was, he needed to move quickly through the night to gain as much distance as possible before daylight forced him to hide again.

Gritting his teeth, Dirge set off once more. When the pain got too bad, he would think of all the tunes he had played on his oboe, not knowing if they had been learned, or if he'd made them up, and the dancing notes in his head took his mind off the pain, indeed, after a while he found himself humming little counter melodies to the tunes he had played. In this way, he walked much faster than otherwise might have done, and was startled to see, just as the morning light turned the sky pink and gold, a black fence (with five bars going horizontally and one coming down every so often) stretching out in front of him.

Not caring whether he was observed or not, Dirge scrambled towards it, only seeing it as the end of his journey - the end of the terrible wood in which he had been forced to live for who knew how long?

Using the last of his strength, Dirge forced himself to climb over the Bar Barrier, sobbing with pain, until he reached the safety of a clump of bushes on the far side of the little lane that ran along there.

His last conscious thought was, now that he was out of the wood, he was safe from Dee Sharp.

Dirge stumbled into the bushes (where, had he but known it, Crumhorn and Sackbut had hidden when <u>they</u> first arrived!) and fell, unconscious, drained by his dramatic escape!

CHAPTER 4

Fanfare gently patted Materlinck's wing, as the bluebird settled himself down for a nap: Mahler was already asleep.

Fanfare rose and went round checking on the rest of the creatures. One of the Inspiration Sprites was looking a little off-colour. His healthy bright blue glow had dimmed to a dismal grey, and the other Sprites were clearly concerned about him.

Fanfare wished, yet again, that the Maestro had been able to return to Scores Hall, but in the last message he'd had, Monody had told him on no account was he to risk the bluebirds, (he didn't need to be told <u>that</u> twice!) as the robins who had been sent with messages had died after being caught in the… what was it?… ah, yes the Woodwind.

The message had been short, obviously written in haste, and although the robin who'd delivered it had, by some miracle, survived, Fanfare intended to obey his master's instructions to the letter. <u>None</u> of the magical creatures were to be sent out until Monody, himself, gave them the go-ahead. He'd ended the note by saying that he and Forlana were organising things at Cadence Falls, where he would remain for the foreseeable future.

Fanfare had rushed to tell the Circle of Five - the secret group that met in the little hidden room behind one of the studies. Professors Cloche, Tamburo, and Madame Leider had immediately stepped up, saying that they would take on the Maestro's duties temporarily, if Fanfare wouldn't mind devoting himself solely to looking after the magical creatures, (As this was exactly what the little herald was hoping for, he was quick to agree!)

They would just have to cope as best they could until the Maestro was able to return.

Telling the sprites to let him know if there was any change in their friend, Fanfare turned to leave the large barn to check on supplies, when a rustling behind him stopped him in his tracks.

He knew who it was before he turned around.

"Yes, Scales, what can I do for you?"

"Well, I've been thinking…" Scales began, slowly.

"Oh do get on with it, Scales - I have far too much to do…" The little herald stopped as he saw the hurt expression in the dragon's eyes.

"I'm sorry… we're all a bit tense at the moment. Now, what do you want?"

"I want to help; I can do things the others can't!" Scales said in a rush, afraid that if he paused again, Fanfare would go.

Indeed, barely listening to him, Fanfare was nearly out the door, when he turned and said, "<u>What</u> can you do?"

"The evil, the sadness-thingy, it doesn't affect me."

"Nonsense!" began Fanfare, testily.

"It's true!" insisted the little dragon. "Remember when Faye and the Inspiration Sprites were captured by Dee Sharp?"

Fanfare shuddered; that had been a terrible time - that had been a terrible time - they'd nearly <u>lost</u> <u>both</u> the Sprites, <u>and</u> Faye (who'd become seriously ill after spending too much time in Octavia.) Indeed, Fledermaus, the bat, <u>had</u> died on that mission!

Fanfare nodded, silently.

"Well, I was the diversion - I had to fly <u>into</u> the Cacophony Wood from the other side and wait there till Landler and the others came… and then fly out again afterwards… and the sadness didn't affect me one bit!"

Fanfare looked at the little dragon as if seeing him properly for the first time.

"Scales, are you saying you'd be willing to fly, <u>knowing</u> that the Woodwind could appear at any time?"

"Yes!" Scales was pleased to see he understood. "I've heard people talking… Everyone is worried because we don't know where this Woodwind is, or when it will come. I thought I could fly out in a different direction each day… and <u>see</u> where it is!"

Fanfare sighed. "It <u>is</u> a good plan, Scales, but the Maestro said <u>no</u> magical creatures were to go outside…"

"Yes, because they'd get sick, but I <u>won't</u>, because I didn't last time."

It was too tempting an offer… they <u>needed</u> to know where the Woodwind was; but Fanfare still wanted a precaution in place, first.

"Can you flame?"

"Er… yes… the Maestro explained what I'd have to do to

produce flame."

"And you've tried it?"

"Well, no... I mean, I'd need Flame Rocks, and they're only found in the Crescendo Range." The little dragon moved his head in the direction of the huge mountains that could be seen rising up into the clouds.

Fanfare sighed, shook himself, then came to a decision.

"I'm not promising anything, Scales, but... if you're <u>sure</u> you want to do this... tomorrow you may fly to the Crescendo Range and collect a supply of Flame Rocks; I'll give you some sacks to carry them back in. <u>If</u> you can produce a good enough flame, (you'll need it to destroy any Woodwind that crosses your path) and <u>if</u> I can convince Professor Tamburo that you won't come to any harm... you can go on a <u>short</u> mission to locate the Woodwind!"

Scales flapped his wings happily, then said, with a puzzled look, "Professor Tamburo?"

Fanfare bit his lip: of course, Scales didn't <u>know</u> about the Circle - he <u>must</u> be more careful!

Continuing smoothly, he said, "Yes, of course. With the Maestro away, Tamburo is the most senior professor here - naturally, I must run it past him, first."

The little dragon accepted this explanation without question, much to Fanfare's relief, so having told Scales to go and have a good meal, then get some sleep, Fanfare set off to find Tamburo.

It didn't take long to find him, for as soon as Fanfare had made his way back to the main corridor, he could hear the big timpani drums being pounded rhythmically, as one of the students was practising Gustow Holst's 'The Planets' Suite.

Not wanting to disturb the professor during a rehearsal, Fanfare waited outside until the drumming stopped, and a few minutes later, Hoop, a student with a mop of red hair, stumbled out, looking exhausted.

"Not bad," Tamburo called after him, "but practise that second entry - it was late!"

"Yes, professor." Hoop called back as he disappeared round the corner.

Fanfare tapped on the open door, and went in.

Tamburo turned, frowning, but when he saw it was not another student, his brows lifted.

"Fanfare! Everything alright?"

"I <u>think</u> so, Professor Tamburo, but I did need to have a quick word."

Tamburo indicated a drum stool, and Fanfare sat down.

By the time he'd outlined Scales' plan, Tamburo's mobile face had at first frowned in denial, then looked surprised and was now set in thoughtful lines as he mulled over what the herald had said.

"And he knows how to flame?"

"Well, yes," replied Fanfare, slightly less than truthfully, "he is a dragon, after all!"

"Hmm - he is the only dragon… now." Tamburo murmured. He was old enough to just about remember, when he was a little lad, that there had been many dragons living in the Crescendo Range.

His father had been a professor at Scores Hall, too, so he had grown up listening to the dragons roaring at sunset; the sound had echoed and grown louder as it travelled up the vast mountains into the open air above, and by the time it reached their ears, it was loud enough to drown out every lesson in the hall, so that it became the signal to end work for the day. It was so much a part of his life, that Tamburo couldn't recall exactly how old he was when it suddenly stopped. After the third day of silence, a party was sent into the Range to see if the dragons were alright. The Music Fairies returned to the hall with the most extraordinary news… the dragons were gone! Not ill, not dying… just vanished! It was only as the search party was about to leave that Piccolo happened to spot a mottled purple egg which had somehow rolled away and settled on a narrow ledge.

Having managed to rescue it and carefully secure it to his Beamer, Piccolo decided the best thing to do would be to take it back to Scores Hall and give it to the Maestro, (a newly-appointed Monody.)

He had at once agreed that Piccolo had done the right thing - they couldn't leave the egg up there alone, as they had no idea when the dragons would return so Monody consulted the ancient books in the library and made sure the egg was correctly placed and heated.

Indeed, Monody was next to it, several days later, when it suddenly hatched… and out sprang a baby dragon! Most Music Dragons were in shades of pale lilac, or blue through to a deep purple, but this little dragon was black and white all over - a thing Monody had never seen before, although there was a faint lilac tinge, just under the white. As the markings resembled piano keys, Monody names him Scales, only realising later on that, of course, dragons were also covered in scales!

The little dragon quickly grew attached to the Maestro, so it was agreed that Monody and Fanfare should raise him at the hall.

Tamburo brought himself back to the present with a shake.

"Are we right to risk the <u>only</u> dragon we've got?" He looked worriedly at Fanfare.

"He's <u>very</u> certain he can do it!" Fanfare said, earnestly.

"Well, then," Tamburo pushed himself off the drum stool he was sat on, "we'd better go to the Maestro's study, take a look at the maps and plot a course for him. When will he be ready to leave?"

"As soon as he's been to the Crescendo Range to collect some Flame Rock," Fanfare replied with more confidence than he felt.

Tamburo opened the door and took a quick look outside.

"Coasts clear; come on, best that no one else knows about this until Scales returns with some information!"

Fanfare nodded. He hoped the Maestro would forgive him for disobeying a direct order, but they needed to know <u>where</u> the Woodwind was; their very survival might depend on it!

CHAPTER 5

Dee Sharp awoke with a start, and, for a moment, couldn't make out where she was; however, as she glanced round the shambolic mess that filled her bedchamber, it all came flooding back far too clearly.

The day before had begun in its usual way - she'd woken up, completed her ablutions, then gone to check on her potions, and to see if her pet crow had returned with news. It hadn't, so she decided to have breakfast whilst waiting for the bird.

She rang for Dirge... nothing happened. Impatient as ever, she went to the door and called down, "DIRGE! Where are you? I want my breakfast!" She waited for the faint 'I'm coming, Madam,' which usually meant he would take an age limping up the stairs... and still, nothing. That limp of his really annoyed her... she'd done her best to tend to his leg when she'd found him, all those years ago, and yet that stupid limp had never gone away... well, it certainly wasn't <u>her</u> fault that he was so slow with everything. To be honest, he was hardly worth keeping around, and if he didn't arrive soon, she would threaten him with banishment the next time she saw him. <u>That</u> ought to scare him into doing his job properly!

A thought suddenly occurred to her - suppose he had somehow fallen and was lying unconscious downstairs! She started down the stone steps, calling out occasionally, opening a door here and there.

The enchantress had no finer feelings; she wasn't doing this out of <u>concern</u> for Dirge, she was merely irritated that he hadn't come to do her bidding.

At the door of his room, she knocked. No answer. She opened it and peered inside. The shabby make-shift bed looked as though it hadn't been slept in, so she concluded that if Dirge <u>had</u> met with an accident, he had done so yesterday evening, after she'd gone to bed.

It took her some hours to scour the castle, and by the time she'd done a thorough search, Dee Sharp had finally come to the conclusion that, for whatever reason, her servant had gone into the woods!

Having no interest in anyone but herself, she'd never bothered to enquire of Dirge what he did when he wasn't serving her; he was just always there when she required anything!

When she finally came back to the turret room in which her potions were laid out, a black feather on the floor told her the crow had flown in with a report, but finding no one there, the stupid bird had flown off again, instead of waiting for her! This did nothing to improve her temper, and, as always, when she was angry her first instinct was to destroy. But not in this room, where her precious potions were!

She went to her rooms on the floor above and spent an hour hurling things about. When all that could be smashed lay about her feet, she came to a decision. She only had two Discords left, (Brio having destroyed the other three) and though she had sent them out time and time again to collect the angry, discarded Dots that found their way into the wood from a Cascade or Deluge, recently they had always returned with nothing: another incidence that irritated her greatly for, without the Dots she could create no more Discords!

But now, anger made her reckless, and she instructed the grey, sickly looking creations to find Dirge, and if he was injured, take note of his location and bring her news… but if he wasn't, well, he would be very sorry indeed!

She sent one out to the East and one to the West. They could only go as far as the Bar Barrier, for her magic could not penetrate it, but they should be able to find him if he was in the wood.

As they left, she was torn between wanting to find something to eat, as she was very hungry by now, and wanting to wait in the turret room for the crow to return… hunger won.

Upon entering the kitchen, she was surprised to see how little food there was in it. A few uncooked roots lay in a bowl next to the sink - a single apple sat on a shelf, as if forgotten, and half a dozen berries were scattered across the table as if they'd fallen off a plate. She could find nothing else, as she knew nothing of the little lean-to outside.

Scooping everything edible up, she returned to the turret room. It didn't take her long to eat all that she had, and she was still hungry. Fortunately, the crow came back just then, so she forgot about her hunger at once, and quickly went to it.

Staring into the crow's beady black eye, Dee Sharp concentrated hard. A picture began to form in her mind. A small village went about its daily business, when suddenly, it was enveloped in a swirling, green mist. Dee Sharp watched delightedly as, first one, then another Fairy staggered, then fell... and lay still. She shrieked with glee, startling the crow, who tried to take flight, but her cruel fingers gripped it hard round the throat and the crow kept still.

Fairies were fleeing now, running and flying this way and that in their panic. One knelt by a fallen friend, then tried to rise, but it was too late, and they, too, collapsed.

The crow shook itself and the vision disappeared.

Furious, Dee Sharp went to dash the bird against the stone wall, when she suddenly changed her mind.

"What of the other direction? Show me where the other mist went!"

The crow, once so cocky, was finding out exactly how ruthless and evil the enchantress was!

No more stroking of feathers or being fed treats - the crow knew it would be lucky to escape with its life, however it had no choice but to show her what it had seen in the other direction.

Dee Sharp peered into the vision, searching for any signs of Fairies suffocating, but all she could see was the swirling green mist, travelling lazily along, and occasionally, when there was a gap, she could see greenery below, stretching out, which meant there were no dwellings in that particular place.

Screaming with frustration, she went to hurl the crow from her, but luckily, the bird was ready for it, and, once released, gave a huge twist in mid-air, narrowly escaping the wall and diving, instead, out of the open window. (It flew clean out of the Cacophony Wood before it dared stop for a rest.)

Dee Sharp flung herself into a chair. Only <u>one</u> of her spells had brought about the disaster she so craved. She wished the potion wasn't so difficult to create - it took time and effort, and the slightest mistake would render it useless! She would have to check all her ingredients again to see if she had everything she needed to make more.

The enchantress spent some time, carefully going through her supplies, her potions and the last few ingredients needed to create the evil green mist.

Yes!

She had everything she needed!

The second green twig the crow had brought her sat in a small vial of water. Once it had been used, she knew it would be <u>very</u> difficult to locate another, unless that crow was so stupid that it came back again for further instructions, but, after her treatment of it, she thought it probably wouldn't, which was more annoying than everything else!

She was just laying the last of the ingredients carefully to one side, in order of their addition to the mixture, when she heard the familiar sounds of the Discords returning. She ran down all seven flights of stairs in her haste to reach them.

As she went out into the courtyard at the front of the castle, the first thing she noticed was that neither Discord bore any sign that they had found Dirge. No hastily scribbled note, no scrap of his clothing.

Dee Sharp stared hard at first one, then the other monstrous creation - she had given them a <u>very</u> limited intelligence; just enough so that they were able to obey simple instructions, so it didn't take her very long to discover that they had found no trace of Dirge whatsoever.

She automatically sent them on a patrol to look for other Discarded Dots, one to the South, and one to the North, but she knew that Dirge would find the mountain ridge, which lay North behind the castle, impossible to climb, while to the South there were dense, thorny bushes which formed an impossible thicket, so she had very little hope that her retainer would be found in either location.

As the Discords left on their new errands, Dee Sharp walked slowly back into the castle. If the Discords had not found Dirge there could only be one reason… Dirge didn't <u>want</u> to be found! There had been <u>no</u> accident - he wasn't lying helpless and injured somewhere… he had deliberately <u>chosen</u> to leave!

As this realisation dawned on her, Dee Sharp's anger built to new heights, as all her failures returned to haunt her.

First, three of her Discords were destroyed by some unknown force; in some sort of battle. Secondly, her planned capture of the Inspiration Sprites (which was brilliant!) had been defeated by a girl on a bat! True, she had snatched the magic bracelet, the means of which the child could travel between worlds, before the girl escaped and Dee Sharp got burned.

However, her plan to kidnap a maker of the bracelet had depended on two idiot Goblins who had been her prisoners, being sent into the Fairy villages - it <u>should</u> have worked, but Dee Sharp had shared one of the crows visions which clearly showed that the Goblins had been captured by the Gnomes, and were now, no doubt, in chains in some dungeon or other, where they could be of no more use to her.

And <u>now</u> after all these losses, failures and hardships, Dirge whom <u>she'd</u> reduced, cared for, fed and clothed, had, for no reason she could fathom, deserted her and was, this very minute, she had no doubt, seeking to ally himself with her sworn enemies - the Music Fairies!

Two hours later, once she had destroyed virtually everything in the castle, Dee Sharp, with a new calmness, walked back into the turret room, to create enough green mist to kill them all... including Dirge!

CHAPTER 6

Forlana, sitting at a makeshift wooden table in Landler's old living room, now the Treatment Centre, finished the pile of labels she had been writing, and stretched to relieve her cramped shoulder, arm and hand muscles.

As she went towards the old kitchen, now the Distillery, the heaving, banging and pounding which she had endured for the last hour, finally stopped.

Glock and Bel were just stepping back to admire their handiwork as she came in.

"Hello, Forlana," Glock said, respectfully touching his cap. "Come to see how we're gettin' on?"

"Er, yes," she replied, hastily, glancing up at the four shelves they had secured to the wall, one of which was decidedly crooked!

"Good job, lads," she went on, in what she hoped was a positive tone, "but... erm... Glock, do you think that one on the left is quite... er... straight?"

Glock peered at it, frowned, then said, "Think so, Forlana, tell you what though..." in demonstration he placed a heavy, glass jar squarely on one end of the shelf and stepped back, just as the jar slid smoothly to the far end, where it would have landed neatly on top of Bel's head, had Forlana not dashed forward and caught it!

"Ooh! Ah, well yes, Forlana, now you come to mention it..."

Glock took the jar from her and put it carefully on the table while Bel, who had been bending down putting his tools away, got up cautiously, looking around for anything else that might pose an unseen threat.

Forlana laughed. "It's alright, Bel, just straighten that shelf up, and nothing else should land on your head!"

"Better his head than a Fairy's, beggin' your pardon, Forlana," Glock said worriedly. "We Gnomes have 'ard 'eds no doubt, but if that jar 'ad landed on a Fairy, well..."

Bel said shyly, "I'm sorry, Forlana, but we've been called on for so many jobs today that, ... well, I might have rushed it a bit."

"It's alright, Bel, I'm not blaming you. I know how hard <u>all</u> of you are working; it's just jars of medicine there…"

"Say no more, Forlana - we'll fix it now."

Leaving the two Gnomes to re-align the shelf, Forlana went back into the main room to clear the table, wishing for perhaps the tenth time that day that Presto was there, and not at the Red Barn.

Not that she begrudged Rollo and his team there in any way, for she realised how useful Presto would be to them, it was just that, handy as the Gnomes were, they simply didn't have the same skills as Presto did.

Besides, she missed him.

Not being of a romantic disposition, it never once occurred to Forlana to wonder why Presto chose to spend so much time in her company; if anyone had asked, she would have said that he was Landler's friend and, because she and Landler spent a lot of time together, it was only natural that she and Presto would see each other, too.

In fact, Forlana was well aware that Presto was, very slightly, afraid of her, and had used this to her advantage on more than one occasion.

Yes, Forlana decided, <u>that's</u> what she was missing, not Presto, himself, but someone to spar with and tease.

Just then, a quiet tap on the door brought her sharply back to the present and, as she opened it, she gave herself a little shake.

Jig and Reel stood there, both holding a huge pile of small, woven boxes.

"That <u>was</u> quick work! Come in lads - put them on the table."

"Thanks, Forlana. Thought we'd bring round what we've made so far, but there's more to come," Reel said as he emptied his arms onto the table.

"No patterns," Jig said randomly as he put his pile down, too.

Forlana frowned, then glanced at the boxes and understood. Where Jig would normally weave brightly coloured patterns into his baskets and bags, every single box was just one colour.

"So as you can tell what's in 'em," Jig went on. "Like… red for poppy, blue for Lupin and so on."

"Jig, that's a really good idea!" Forlana cried, impressed. "We'll code everything by colour - that'll save a lot of time, thank you!"

"Pleasure," Jig said. "Well, we best get back and make some more!"

"Wait, at least have a drink before you go, lads. You must be thirsty after all that work!"

"Fling and Stem are making 'em too." Reel grinned. "We've left 'em back at mine, still workin'."

"Tell you what - wait here a minute." Forlana went to her cottage next door and soon returned, carrying a large jug.

Reel smiled politely. "Er… Lupin tea?"

"As if!" Forlana laughed. "This is from the stash of Whoops-A-Daisy that Shawm gave to Landler ages ago. Between you and me, Landler's never touched a drop after that first taste!"

Both Gnomes laughed heartily. Their favourite beer was <u>far</u> too strong for Fairies to drink!

"That's more like it!" grinned Jig, taking the jug carefully.

"It's for all <u>four</u> of you!" said Forlana with a mock scowl, "and don't think I won't check with Fling and Stem later!"

"Come and see the shelf, Forlana," Bel stuck his head out of the kitchen. Intrigued, Jig and Reel followed her; and though they couldn't see what was so amusing about an ordinary shelf with a large glass jar sat firmly in the middle of it, Glock and Bel seemed to be very happy with it, and were pleased to be invited back to Reels for lunch, having spotted the jug in Jig's hands.

Forlana saw them all off, then returned to her list of things to do and ticked off 'SHELVES'.

***

Meanwhile, in the fields just beyond the Pizzicato Pool, four figures could be seen, cutting and collecting a variety of flowers, herbs and plants which grew there.

They seemed to be an unlikely group of friends, consisting of two Music Fairies, a Gnome and a Goblin, but the lively chatter and occasional laughter that floated on the air showed how well they were getting along.

Lakme and Mallika both had skills in knowing which flora made the best remedies, and were working together, a little way off from the other two.

"No, not <u>that</u> one, Sackbut - look at the petals; they're different shapes, see?"

"Oh, yes. Sorry, Lilt… is this one right?"

"Yes! That's it; now, cut it just below the leaves - that's it! Any more there?"

"Yes, lots. How many do you want?"

"About half of what's there. We <u>never</u> take it all - it has to be free to grow."

Sackbut nodded. He was learning such a lot. He put the cut plants into the bag he carried, and looked around. His life couldn't be more different now from what it had been. He tried never to think of the dungeons where he and Crumhorn had been held, the prisoners of Dee Sharp, for so long.

And now, despite the fact that they had been guilty of kidnapping one of the most popular Fairies in Cadence Falls, they were free, thanks to Polka, herself, who insisted that they'd been punished enough. So now, out of gratitude to her, Sackbut was doing his very best to be as similar to the Gnomes and Music Fairies as he could, and slowly but surely, it was working.

Suddenly, a beautiful sound filled the air - Sackbut looked up, expecting to see Fairies flying overhead… but there was no one in sight.

"The Ondulandi!" Lakme cried across to them. "Come on!"

She and Mallika raced back the way they had come, so Lilt and Sackbut followed suit.

The party halted a little way from the bank and sat down quietly to listen.

The two Fairies, who had heard them play many times, smiled and closed their eyes as they listen; Lilt, who had heard the music from a distance before, watched with interest, but Sackbut sat, completely entranced, eyes wide and mouth open, caught up in this totally new experience.

The beautiful Water Sprites, with their pale green skin and long turquoise hair were the most entrancing creatures the Goblin had ever seen. They all played on delicate harps, and before long, Sackbut found himself crying, without knowing why, and as the music came to an end, he whispered, "Don't go."

Lilt sighed, as if releasing himself from their spell. "They play every day, Sackbut."

"Every day? When can we come again?"

"I don't know - when there's time… but we <u>will</u>, I promise."

The Ondulandi were disappearing beneath the pool, as the party of four got up and prepared to walk back to Cadence Falls, but Lakme suddenly saw two Sprites break away from the others and swim towards them.

"Stay here," she whispered, as Lilt and Sackbut came to join them. "I'll see what they want. It must be important - they don't usually speak to anyone they don't know really well."

Lakme made her way down to the water's edge and, knowing some of the Ondulandi's ways, bowed very formally.

The two Ondulandi looked at each other, nodded, then bowed to Lakme. The shorter one lifted her hands out of the water, and Lakme could see she held a beautiful and very unusual looking flower in her hands.

Despite Lakme's considerable knowledge, she had never seen a bloom like this before.

Although it sat, open-petalled like a lily, the petals themselves were more poppy-shaped; the tips were white, gradually becoming pale, then deeper blue, until at last, the stamen in the centre was a rich, royal blue.

As the Sprite raised her hands Lakme reached out to take the flower, and nearly dropped it as the girl, in a strange, other-worldly voice said one word…

"FOR-LA-NA!"

CHAPTER 7

Dal, Catch and Glee wandered up the path that ran parallel to the Bar Barrier, though after an excellent lunch of stew and 'taters, their pace was a little slower than it had been that morning.

"It's all very well," Dal was saying, "for Souza to come and tell us he needs Shawm and Lute on patrol, but who's gonna 'elp us do all the 'eavy liftin', that's what I'd like to know!"

Catch and Glee, somewhat younger than Dal, smothered a laugh: So far, all that Dal had been required to carry that day was a couple of straw pallets, a pile of blankets and four pillows.

Catch, Glee and Lute had actually done the heavy stuff, loading spare beds, chairs and cupboards onto Presto's cart which he'd left, luckily, at the Warehouse.

It had been Dal's idea to come up this route, as he was old enough to remember the abandoned Gnome-Home, about half a mile away. (This was <u>not</u> the dwelling where Crumhorn and Sackbut had held Polka captive, but another one further along which, had the Goblins but known it, was a lot sturdier and drier than the one <u>they</u> had found!)

When Cadence Falls had first been built, to deal with the Cascades and rejected Dots, there had been a small colony of Gnomes living on what became the outskirts of the new village.

Over time, the Gnomes had got to know and make friends with the Music Fairies who came to live there. Gradually, the Gnomes moved into the new cottages that lay at the bottom of the first hill, close to the waterfall, so that they were always on hand to collect the Dots and take them to the recently-built Warehouse.

Eventually, the old Gnome-Homes fell into a dilapidated state and were left behind.

Dale had the idea that some bits and bobs of old furniture may still be there, which could be useful.

They'd just rounded the corner and were passing a clump of

bushes that grew there, when Glee said, "What's that?"

They all came to a halt.

"Listen!" said Glee. "There it is again!"

A low, but audible moan came from their left.

As one, they all moved to the bushes, and there, laying on his side, was an unconscious figure!

"Quick, Glee - feel for a pulse!"

Glee knelt down, then glared up at Dal, "Of course he'll have a pulse - he's moanin'!" But Glee took the wrist in his fingers anyway, counted, and nodded.

"Must have knocked hisself out somehow," Catch said, looking around for a heavy object, and found nothing.

Glee got up swiftly. "Maybe he's sick! You know, that whirlwind thing!"

"Woodwind," Dal corrected him. "Aye, could be, but it's not come 'ere yet?"

The three Gnomes looked at each other, dubiously.

"Tell you what," Dal said, at length, "reckon you two had better go and get Presto's cart. We'll take 'im to the Warehouse. Less'n you think we can push 'im all the way to the Treatment Centre?"

Catch and Glee looked at each other, then shook their heads.

"Not up and down them two big 'ills, Dal... s'posin' we dropped 'im?" Catch said in a panic.

"That's what I thought," Dal nodded in agreement.

"Warehouse it is. Forlana can take a look at 'im there."

It didn't take Catch and Glee too long to come back with the empty cart.

The three Gnomes pushed it along carefully, Dal at one side, ready to grab at the patient if he started to slide.

"Tell you what, lads. I reckon we'd best put 'im in that little room with the curtain across it, you know, where we used to store the supplies, before we 'ad a proper kitchen."

"Why?" asked Catch.

"Well," Dal lowered his voice to a whisper and said, "until Forlana's taken a look at 'im, we won't know if it's sommat <u>we</u> can get, with me?"

The other two looked at him, then, ever so slightly, sped up until they reached the Warehouse.

Having seen their charge onto a wooden pallet and found him a pillow and a couple of blankets, all three Gomes went and had a good wash under the pump, just in case!

***

Forlana, balancing two large boxes on her knee, closed the door to Landler and Polka's new cottage and crossed the street to the Treatment Centre, where she'd left the door open, knowing she'd have her hands full on the way back!

In the middle of the night, being unable to sleep, she'd suddenly remembered that, the day before the Handclasping, Presto had asked her where he should put the boxes of dried herbs that Polka had collected. Trying to organise several things at once, Forlana had retorted abruptly, "Oh! Put them anywhere!"
And so, he had… in the guest room, under the bed! It had taken her nearly an hour to find them, (during which time she'd invented a lot of new names for Presto!) so she was not surprised, on her return, to find five messages waiting for her.
Sighing, she went to put the herbs in the Distillery, and nearly dropped both boxes when she saw the vase by the sink.
Crossing to it, she picked up the unusual bloom that sat in the water and whispered, "The Perdendo Poppy - I must find the Maestro!"

***

Glee panted as he started up the second hill - he <u>had</u> to find either Forlana or the Maestro; they had no idea what was wrong with the stranger, and they needed advice!
Glee had his head down, and so did not see the Fairy careering towards him… until they collided!
Forlana, being the lighter of the two, came off worse: she went flying onto the ground, and as for Glee, he was positively quaking

in his boots when he realised who he'd knocked down!

"Oh, my! F… F… Forlana… I'm… I'm so sorry! I was just coming to find you."

"Well, here I am! What's so important?" She scowled at him, rubbing her head and then her knee.

"We've found someone. He's knocked out and in a terrible state - we took 'im to the ware'ouse, it bein' closest, but we don't know if he's cong… congat…"

Forlana frowned for a moment, then the penny dropped.

"You mean 'contagious'."

"Thass what Dal said!" Glee was relieved to see she understood.

"Yes! Will you come?" The Gnome continued as he picked her up.

"Um… yes, I think I must, but as soon as I've done that, I must find the Maestro!"

"Good idea - he'll know what's what," Glee replied, misunderstanding her.

At the Warehouse they both went into the small curtained-off area where the Gnomes had lain their patient on a make-shift pallet.

Dal looked up as they came in.

"Ah, Forlana! Good. We've kept 'im away from the others, just in case. We reckon 'e might 'ave come from Galliard or Bagatelle, you know? Saw that mist from a distance - like, and decided to trek 'ere, rather than go straight into it. Dunno why 'e won't wake up, though," Dal finished, scratching his head.

"I'll take a look at him, Dal. You did the right thing, bringing him here; well done, lads!" Her smile encompassed all three of them. "Now, if you could give me a bit of room?"

"Come on, lads, we've still got more beds and pallets to find." Dal and the other two bowed and made to leave.

"Ah, Catch, on your way out, please could you see if Ocarina has any stew on the stove for when he wakes up."

"Right away, Forlana!" Catch replied as he left.

Forlana turned back to her patient. He was covered in cuts and bruises and there was dried blood on his face. Forlana frowned - it looked as though he'd been running away from something… or someone! Her frown deepened as she felt for a pulse and noticed how thin his wrist was" She opened the tattered cloak he wore and began to gently turn him this way and that, looking for more serious injuries when, suddenly, as she rolled him onto his side, she gasped! His wings, now on view, were bordered with dark markings and designs, the likes of which Forlana had never seen! At first she wondered if, somehow, the Woodwind had marked him, or if it was a disfigurement caused by the disease which had made him pass out, but once she'd turned him onto his other side, she came to the conclusion that the markings were far too symmetrical for that! Apart from this, Forlana could find no trace of any disease or illness; no rash, no temperature and none of the usual symptoms such as coughing or rapid breathing.

She came to the conclusion that his main problems were malnutrition - not having enough to eat or drink - and exhaustion.

On examining his feet, she'd found he'd walked the soles almost off his boots and his feet were cut and bleeding. Wrapping his cloak tightly round him again, and covering him with a blanket, but leaving his feet bare, Forlana went out to find Ocarina. She asked the Fairy to bathe and bandage the patient's feet and to send someone to find her the second he woke up!

This done, she set off back up the double hills again so see if the Maestro had returned to the Treatment Centre; she had two reasons to find him now!

Forlana decided to fly up the two hills, and walk down the other side. She had often wanted to ask the Maestro why the Music Fairies had wings, when they rarely used them" She'd seen pictures, as a youngling, of other kinds of Fairies, such as the Weather Sprites or the Flora and Fauna Fairies and they all seemed to have much bigger and more powerful wings.

Theirs were fine for short flights, such as when she and Polka had brought Faye between them, from the Mezzo Meadow to Cadence Falls on her first visit, or when the whole village flew to the Festival Fields for a celebration, but the Music Fairies couldn't do sustained flying. Added to which, they couldn't fly at all after they'd been for a dip in the Pizzicato Pool, until their wings were dry!

It had often puzzled her, and she would ask - one day - but now, she had more important things to think about.

Forlana opened the door to the Treatment Centre (which had now been closed) and went in, calling, "Maestro?"

No answer came but, as she went into the Distillery, she noticed that the Perdendo Poppy was gone, and in its place was a note that simply read:

'Gone to see the Ondulandi. M.'

'Well, at least that's <u>one</u> problem dealt with!' Thought Forlana as she started to unpack all the dried herbs. 'The other will just have to wait for the Maestro's return.'

CHAPTER 8

The bright little duet danced merrily to its conclusion and the two musicians glanced at each other before sighing and crossing to slump down on the other side of the room, backs against the sofa.

"Nothing... again!" Faye said miserably, holding her Clef Crystal out in front of her eyes.

"I know," replied Peri, who was doing exactly the same thing with hers.

It had been nearly six weeks, (in their time) since they had come back from Octavia; forced to leave all their friends facing this new, evil green 'Woodwind', (the Maestro's name for it) and <u>now</u>, they had no idea how any of the Music Fairies were - if they were safe, or if they needed help, and <u>still</u> the Maestro hadn't called them back!

The one and only good thing that had happened was that they had been putting in hours and hours of practice, not (as their mums thought) because it gave them the chance to spend more time together, but because it had been the Maestro's final instruction to them. "The <u>only</u> way you can help your friends <u>is</u> <u>to</u> <u>practise</u>! I cannot stress that enough!"

Maestro Monody was very rarely that serious with them, but they knew him well enough to know that, for some reason, this was <u>really</u> important!

So, as soon as they'd returned from Octavia, they began to work really hard. They practised alone, and together and at the end-of-year concert (which had come and gone nearly four weeks ago now,) their duet 'The Lark On The Water' was such a success that both Miss Hummingstone and Mr Bridge (who taught Peri the violin) were actually complimentary, instead of the usual "Now, let's look at that passage again shall we, and <u>this</u> time, do <u>try</u> to play what's written."

All the parents had said nice things to the girls that, a few weeks before, would have pleased them very much, but now, they were so worried about the Music Fairies that they smiled and said 'Thank you', but without really taking it in.

Faye also had something else to worry about. Two weeks after the concert, Aunt Laura had been taken ill. Mum had gone to see her as soon as she was able, (leaving Faye at Peri's house) but on her return, it was clear to Faye that the news wasn't good.

"The doctor has said she's too ill to have any visitors for the moment, Faye, so I'm sorry but we won't be able to go over on Sundays for a while."

"Oh," Faye was a little surprised at how upset she felt. At first, she had thought it just a chore that they had to go over for 'tea' every Sunday, but gradually, Faye discovered she was looking forward to it each week, especially when Aunt Laura also invited Peri to come a couple of times.

Aunt Laura would tell them stories of when she, as a young woman, had travelled far and wide, giving concerts and recitals, and the girls found it really interesting.

She had, of course, attended their concert, too, and although she had only said, "Well done girls - but no more than I would expect of you, of course," both the girls could see she was very proud of them and that, somehow, meant more to them than all the other compliments they'd had.

Peri was also sad Aunt Laura was ill. She'd grown to like the old lady when Faye was really ill, and she'd intended to ask her about the Music Fairies when she next saw her.

Nothing seemed to be going right at the moment.

Jenny Martin came in from the kitchen, and the girls looked up.

"Having a rest? Thought so. Here's some milk and a couple of those biscuits I baked last night."

"The orange ones?" Peri said, hopefully.

"Yes!" Jenny smiled. "I know how much you both liked them."

"Thank you!" the girls cried together, as they went to the table.

"Once you've finished, why don't you play that new piece again? What's it called?"

"Skimming Stones," they replied, as one, then looked at each other and burst out laughing.

"That's better," smiled Jenny. "I like to hear you two laughing - you're too young to be sad all the time."

She chatted with them while they had their snack, then she took the tray and went back into the kitchen once more saying mysteriously, "Mrs Norton's 90! fancy that!"

Peri looked at Faye confused.

"Birthday cake order. Mum's just about to start icing it."

Oh, I see!"

The two girls returned to their instruments; Faye to the Piano and Peri to her violin.

They turned their sheet-music back to the beginning, and Faye played the little four bar introduction after which Peri would join in.

Both the girls had agreed, since it was the school holidays, to wear their Clef Crystals <u>all</u> the time now, just in case, but when they came to the end of 'Skimming Stones' once more, they were still there, in Faye's living room, no closer to Landler, Forlana or the Music Fairies then they had been for six long weeks!

***

Landler in fact, was busy making sure that each department in the Red Barn had what it needed for the possible (and probable) siege ahead. The whole place was <u>very</u> efficiently under Rollo's leadership, so once he'd spoken to the Fairies in charge of each section and checked with the Beamer Medics that they weren't short of any supplies, he was free to start putting his own plan into action. He had taken a few minutes out, after communicating with the Medics, to go and check on Brand and Brio. Both were conscious fortunately, and Brand, though weak, was obviously very pleased to see that Landler was alright, and that they'd been rescued in time. Brand then flashed up an image of Polka.

"Yes, Polka's fine too - just a bit of a cough," he thought back to the Beamer, hoping he managed to conceal the anxiety he felt.

He wasn't surprised when, a few seconds later, he caught a weaker image from Brio - he'd been expecting it.

"No, nothing yet. As far as I know, Faye and Peri are still back in their own world. Rollo had a note from the Maestro," (the very last note they'd had,) "and at the end of it all he'd said that the girls had gone back safely, and he wouldn't call them again until needed. That's all I know, Brio. Sorry."

Brio nodded his thanks, then put his head down, too weary to stay awake any longer. When he looked, Brand was already asleep.

Well, they were in the best place, thought Landler, as he went back to find a team of his own.

As luck would have it, three Fairies were just leaving the table after a quick snack, when he reached the main barn. Landler quickly crossed over to them.

"Volta! Roco! Are you busy?"

"Hello, Landler! Are you alright? We heard about your rescue! That was a bit close, wasn't it?"

"Too close!" said Landler, thinking of the Beamers.

"You know Corona, don't you?" Rocco went on, indicating the third Fairy, who was tall and slender with long, golden hair.

"Yes, of course!" Landler wracked his brain, trying to think if he'd met her before.

She smiled. "Of course you don't know me, Landler! We've never met. Me and my mate, Canto, have only been here a little while. We're trying to grow some new hybrid plants that will heal wounds quicker, if the Brigade Guards get injured during a Cascade, you know..." She trailed off as, too late, she remembered the stories she'd heard of Landler's horrific injuries in the Deluge.

It was his turn to smile. "That's alright, Corona. I can tell you this - if you can find something to speed up the healing process, we'll <u>all</u> be in your debt!"

She was saved from any further embarrassment by Canto, who came up at that moment, looking for her.

By the time he had been introduced to Landler, Volta and Roco were about to leave, so Landler said quickly, "Are you all busy now, or could any of you spare an hour or two to help me?"

"Of course we'll help!" Roco said, glancing at the others. "What do you need us to do?"

Landler had just finished explaining about the storerooms when Polka came to join them.

"How do you feel?" Landler immediately asked.

"Perfectly alright!" she smiled up at him. "I've finished all I can do in the Distillery for today, so I came out to help you."

"Ah good!" said Volta, before Landler could protest, "Just what we need! Come on, Polka, there's a little storeroom down the end of the corridor I've been itching to sort out - it's a mess! Usually Rollo won't let us tough anything... but <u>now</u>... !"

She grinned mischievously at Landler, over her shoulder as she led Polka away.

Landler gave a rueful shrug and turned back to the others.

"Corona, Canto, please could you start in the opposite room to Volta and Polka - that way we won't be trying to cross over each other with stuff that has to be moved."

"Of course!" The couple followed Polka and her friend out.

"That leaves us," Landler turned to Roco. "I know where I want to start! Follow me."

He led the other Fairy to the storage room where he had found the 'bubbles' - round glass orbs that resembled goldfish bowls, except they had an opening top and bottom, and were capable of being screwed together by means of a thread at each end.

Landler knew that Rollo had found nearly all the orbs in the Red Barn and turned them into contraptions such as he and Polka had worn to escape Pavane Villa, but he wanted to go through the place carefully, to make sure that none had been overlooked.

He and Roco had been sifting through stuff for nearly an hour, and had only found three more 'bubbles', which Roco had quickly taken to Rollo's workshop) when Viola popped her head round the door.

"Need any help, Landler?"

"Viola - yes! Can you please go and check on Polka, and…"

"I meant with the storerooms," Viola said, with meaning in her expression.

Landler brushed his hair out of his eyes.

"I'm fussing, aren't I?" he said quietly.

"Yes, you are!" Viola came up to him. "It's just a cough, Landler, that's all. I've been in to give her another dose of Buttercup Syrup, and she's fine. I'll start next door, shall I?"

He smiled at her. "Yes please, Viola. I'm sorry - I know Polka doesn't like me fussing."

"Although she'd far too good-natured to say so," came the quiet response as Viola went to the room next door.

Roco came back with the news that Rollo was delighted to have another three orbs, and please could they find some more."

Spending another half an hour searching and stacking boxes neatly, once their contents had been checked, had uncovered no more orbs and Landler was beginning to feel rather dejected.

"The main problem is that we have no means of communicating with anyone!" he exclaimed, as yet another box yielded nothing!

"We've always managed before," Roco was only half-listening as he'd just spied a promising-looking box at the bottom of a pile.

"Yes - but not now!" Landler pushed a box out of the way that landed on the floor, spilling its contents of bronze lamps with enough of a clatter to make Roco look up, startled.

Landler kicked a lamp out of his way, and started pacing up and down; a sure sign that he was agitated.

"We've always been able to use robins or fireflies before - but we can't now. If they get caught in the Woodwind - they <u>die</u>!"

Roco winced.

"Then again, I could always get to whomever I needed to speak with on Brand. The same with the Maestro - Fanfare and his bluebirds would take him wherever he wished to go."

He turned to Roco.

"I flew out of Pavane Villa on Brand - Rollo made him and Brio a sort of mask, but even after <u>that</u> short trip they're ill and exhausted! No, the Maestro won't risk the bluebirds. We have no way of knowing where the Woodwind is - when it's coming here - or even <u>if</u> our friends at Cadence Falls and Scores Hall are alright! And we can do nothing… <u>NOTHING</u>!"

It was at this singularity inopportune moment that Canto came in saying, "Corona and I have just found a box of fireworks - we're not sure where to store them."

"Oh, put them where you like Canto - we've nothing to celebrate!"

CHAPTER 9

Forlana closed the door to her cottage and set off up the hill. She'd decided she'd better see if the Maestro had called in at the Warehouse on his way back from visiting the Ondulandi.

She wasn't altogether surprised when, coming over the crest of the hill, she spotted the Maestro walking downhill towards her. As the two people in charge of running things during this crisis, it was only natural that they would seek each other's opinion when something important or unusual happened.

They both took a breath, and in the same instant called out, "I've been looking for you!"

Laughing together, they met outside Jig and Reel's adjacent cottages, where a small oak bench nestled against the wall.

They both sat down at the same moment, but Forlana, as always, got in first.

"What happened with the Ondulandi, Maestro?"

"You saw the Perdendo Poppy?" he countered with another question.

"Yes - it's one of the reasons I was looking for you!"

"Well, the flower was originally meant for _you_! They didn't know I was here, of course. I hope I didn't overstep my authority here, Forlana."

"Of course not, Maestro! You'll make a much better job of it." she paused, then glanced up at him. "The Olani?"

He nodded, sadly. "She has served her people very well for a long time, but now she must fade away and die, as must we all, one day. I have been asked to return in two hours when three candidates will be presented to me; I must then choose the one _I_ think will make the best new leader... the Olani has already indicated _her_ preference. If we both agree, the new Olani will be inducted as the old one dies; if not, three new candidates will be chosen, and the process will begin again."

Forlana nodded. Fairy folk normally lived for a _very_ long time and in <u>her</u> life-time, Forlana had only known of four Diminuendos (the process by which the Music Fairies came to an end. Each species was slightly different.) and even though the Olani was very old, and Forlana had never met her, she still felt sad at her passing.

The Maestro watched her for a moment, then said, gently: "<u>One</u> of the reasons?"

Forlana looked up, perplexed.

"You said, 'it's <u>one</u> of the reasons I was looking for you'."

Forlana gasped. "Oh, yes! Goodness, I nearly forgot. When they were out, Dal, Catch and Glee discovered a stranger, lying unconscious in a hedge! They took him to the Warehouse, being the closest place, and called me, but when I went to examine him, there's something wrong with his wings! I've never seen it before, but there are all these dark markings down the edges! You don't suppose it's contagious, do you?"

The Maestro frowned. "I wouldn't think so, Forlana. <u>Where</u> did Dal and the others find him?"

"It was as they were walking up to the old abandoned Gnome-Homes; apparently Dal had some idea there might have been some furniture left behind there. I don't know where exactly, but on that path."

"I see. I suppose he <u>could</u> have walked from Galliard, but it's a long trek."

"That's what Dal thought, but if he's come from there, might the Woodwind have got him, just a bit, and done that damage to his wings? Ocarina and Marcato are in the Warehouse all the time, now; we can't risk them getting sick, too!"

"No, indeed!" Monody rose and offered an arm to Forlana, indicating that they should walk down to the Warehouse.

"From the very little I understand about this Woodwind, I believe it kills Fairies by swamping them with sorrow and listlessness, so that they just lose the will to live - it's very quick, by all accounts. No one in their messages has mentioned damaged wings, so I think we may rest easy on that score."

"It's the not knowing that worries me, Maestro. How long before it gets here? Who will be outside when it comes? How long will we be trapped in the Warehouse and… how many of us will survive?" she ended quietly.

The Maestro squeezed her hand.

"If I knew the answer to <u>any</u> of those questions, my dear, I would tell you. But I'm afraid I know as little as you. All we can do is to prepare as best we can and be aware of the danger."

She smiled shakily at him, then followed him round the corner and into the Warehouse.

"Now, my dear, would you be so kind as to deal with the mountain of folk I can see about to ask me questions, while I go and take a look at our patient."

"Of course, Maestro."

Forlana went forward and called the whole group to a nearby table, grabbing paper and pen as she did so, to make a list of all their requests.

Monody seized his chance, and slipped quietly behind the curtain, while all eyes were on Forlana.

The patient lay, still and sleeping. The Maestro went up to him and, as Glee and Forlana had done before him, checked his pulse and put a hand on his forehead. He was hot, there was no doubt about that, running a slight fever, but that could just as easily be due to spending time out in the cold, damp night, as to anything the Woodwind may have done to him.

Monody gently lowered the blankets and opened his cloak, then gasped at what he saw! He knew only too well what those markings were! (There were only a handful of Fairies who did!) And he didn't want to tell Forlana, not yet... not until he was <u>sure</u>!

He covered the wings up again, quickly. He'd make certain to tell Ocarina that the patient's cloak mustn't be removed, not yet.

Monody stared into the sleeping face, looking this way and that, trying to decide what the Fairy would have looked like before pain-lines had etched deep sorrow into his expression, even in his sleep.

The Maestro went to tuck the blankets under his feet, then saw they had been left exposed for a reason. He recognised, at once, Minima's neat bandaging over both feet, but one was still seeping a little blood through the bandage, giving an idea of how very far this poor soul must have walked. On impulse, Monody carefully lifted the blanket to reveal both legs. He nodded at what he saw there...

Several moments later, the Maestro came quietly out of the curtained area, and spotted Dash and Crumhorn sipping a hot Lupin tea, having just come back from a watch at the Falls.

He made his way over to them.

"Hello, lads. I wonder, could you spare a little time to do something for me? I know you've just been on watch..."

"That's alright, Maestro. We can do anything you need, can't we, Crumhorn?"

"Of course, Maestro!" Crumhorn bowed to him.

"Thanks, both of you. Well, you'll have heard there's a patient in the little room over there?"

Both of them nodded.

"He's on a pallet on the floor at present, but I'd rather have him in a bed. Could you take Presto's cart up to the Treatment Centre and bring one back, with bedding, and if it's not too much trouble, please could you also get some Willowbark and Feverfew from the Distillery?"

"Right away, Maestro!" Dash replied cheerfully, slapping Crumhorn on the shoulder.

"Thanks, lads," Monody called after them as they disappeared round the corner to where the cart was stood.

Forlana was just gathering up the sheaf of papers that she'd hastily scribbled everyone's questions and requests on, so Monody went over to the table and sat opposite her.

Forlana glanced around to make sure they wouldn't be overheard.

"Well? What do you think?"

"I don't believe he's contagious," Monody said calmly.

"But his wings!" Forlana was not convinced.

"Forlana, do you trust me?"

"Of course, Maestro!"

"Well, then I must ask you to be patient a little while longer. Once we can find out a bit more about him, I will explain everything to you… agreed?"

She gave a rueful laugh. "Agreed! After all, I'm <u>known</u> for my patience!"

He laughed with her.

"You'll just have to try hard, my dear. And now," he said, rising and stretching out a hand, "I'd better see if I can answer <u>any</u> of these favourably!"

Forlana gave him the lists.

"Could I ask you to remain here until my return, for, as well as dealing with these, I must go back to the Ondulandi."

She nodded.

"When Dash and Crumhorn get back with the bed, could you ask four of the stronger Gnomes to set it up and move him <u>gently</u> onto it. I want him kept where he is, for the present. Oh, and, Forlana, <u>if</u> he wakes up, I need to know… immediately!

CHAPTER 10

After a night's sleep troubled by vague dreams, vivid nightmares and shapeless warnings, Dee Sharp awoke feeling as if she'd not slept at all! She dressed and made a half-hearted attempt to brush her matted hair. Since she had become obsessed with the Woodwind, she'd ceased to worry about taking care of herself, and if she could have glanced in a mirror, she would have been astonished at how old, dirty and dishevelled she looked!

But of course, after ripping off her bandages in frustration when yet another one of her plans had been foiled by the Music Fairies, she'd smashed every single mirror in the castle.

So now, with matted hair and ravaged face, she went down to the kitchens to find food: there wasn't any.

It had never occurred to ask Dirge <u>how</u> there was always food at mealtimes; he just always brought her <u>something</u>.

She searched the kitchen from top to bottom but, now Dirge was gone, there was nothing in the larder; the neatly stacked containers, woven out of bits of straw, hay or string, that the crows brought back from time to time, were standing empty and, much to her annoyance, every jug, bowl, bottle or pitcher that <u>could</u> hold water was up in her workroom, being used to contain the Woodwind in its first development.

She hadn't meant Dirge to leave them without any drinking vessels when she'd sent him off to find containers!… Idiot! Useless moron! And now, <u>he</u> was gone, too!

She flung the kitchen's back door open so hard that one of its hinges broke and the door listed mournfully to one side, a little like Dirge himself. This did nothing to improve her temper, and she stomped around in the grounds, looking for anything that might grow there that she could eat. Had she changed direction she would, eventually, have stumbled across the little place under the lean-to, where Dirge had so painstakingly grown the few seeds he had got from the birds, but her patience ran out before she could find it, and having given up after a short while, she paced back to the broken door and dragged it shut behind her.

Going to the small barrel in the corridor, she lifted the lid and scooped up some of the rain-water, stopped there and drank for a long time.

Her thirst finally quenched, if not her hunger, she went back to her workroom and there, with a sudden burst of energy, darted forward to snatch something from the floor that had fallen, or been dropped near the window.

After her last remaining crow had departed with precipitous haste, she'd left the window open, just in case he decided to return. The fact that he'd come when the room was empty was not lost on her; he'd obviously not wished to fall into her clutches again, but he <u>had</u> brought her something by way of a parting gift! Three young, green twigs lay on the floor, small budlets just beginning to show. Although her energy, (and therefore her power) was starting to wear… hatred drove her on!

***

The Composition Magician arrived at the Pizzicato Pool just in time to see the Ondulandi rise with their harps to play the daily serenade. He sat on a nearby bank to listen, revelling in the beautiful music though noticing, as he did so, that the interwoven melodies were all in minor keys, giving an overall sadness to the sound, as the Ondulandi knew they would soon lose their Olani.

At the end of the piece, the Water Sprites sank gracefully down into the pool once more, accompanied by the Maestro's sigh as he rose.

Four of them, however, remained behind, and swam towards him. The two who halted a little were obviously the Elders, sent to see that the task was carried out properly, but the two younger sprites swam almost to the bank. At the same moment, all four Ondulandi <u>and</u> the Maestro bowed low and, as they straightened, put their arms out, palms facing upwards in the time-honoured greeting.

The youngest Sprite (who was, in fact, the one to whom Peri had spoken on her underwater adventure) spoke in Ondu, the language of the Sprites, which she knew the Maestro understood.

"Oh, great and powerful Maestro. We expected Forlana, but the Ondulandi are honoured that <u>you</u> would grace us with your presence. Before we begin the Selection Ceremony, may we ask a question?"

The Maestro bowed formally.

"Please would you be so good as to tell us why the Music Fairies no longer come to hear us play, or swim in our pool... have we offended in some way?"

"No, indeed, oh pure and gentle Ondulandi, it is <u>we</u> who is honoured to be allowed to visit your beautiful pool and to listen to your melodious music."

All the Ondulandi bowed at this point, very pleased by the Maestro's formal answer.

"The reason is this, "Monody continued, "we have learned of an evil mist, that we have named the Woodwind, because it originates from the Cacophony Wood. We suspect it to be the creation of Dee Sharp. We do not know when or <u>if</u> it will come this way, but we have been told it reached Galliard and Bagatell and those who were caught in it... have died," he paused, while the four Sprites looked at each other in consternation, then went on, "I would not presume to order, but I do <u>advise</u> you, whilst this threat looms, <u>not</u> to rise to the surface each day."

Aeolina, who spoke for them, after consulting with the others, turned back to Monody.

"We shall have to discuss this in Conclave... and with the new Olani... but we will heed your advice, oh Maestro."

The Master bowed once more. As he looked up again, he noticed the two Elders disappearing to fetch the candidates.

Aeolina swam quickly to the very edge of the pool, beckoned Monody forward, then whispered quickly, "We <u>have</u> to rise to the surface each day to breathe in the open air, but we will not play or sing - just breathe and then dive down." She glanced over her shoulder. "They do not wish me to tell you this: privacy, you understand?"

He nodded graciously. "Thank you, Aeolina. I'll respect your wishes, and if I hear any reports of the Woodwind coming this way, I'll send word."

"Thank you, Maestro."

She quickly swam back to her place, just as the Elders appeared - the three candidates forming a line between them.

Though Monody had never witnessed a Selection Ceremony before, he, as Maestro, had read up on it and knew the formalities well.

So… after a long and <u>very</u> boring speech from one of the Elders, Monody bowed to each female in return. They were not maidens, no longer in the first flower of youth, but neither were they elderly; somewhere in the middle for, with the passing years, comes wisdom.

As Aeolina presented the three, she named each one in turn; a rarity, for the Ondulandi did <u>not</u>, as a rule, share their names with outsiders.

"The Olani had made <u>her</u> choice known to us - she would, therefore, like to see if you agree."

The Maestro looked carefully at each candidate. They all seemed calm and serene, but the one on the right (whose name was Solenne) seemed to have a special quality about her. He was drawn to her in a way that did not occur with the other two.

Mondoy bowed low and said clearly, "I choose Solenne!"

He knew at once that his choice concurred with that of the Olani, by the relief on everyone's faces. They all bowed ceremoniously again, then dived deep into the pool; all but Aeolina, who beckoned the Maestro forward again.

"If we may be of help when this Woodwind comes, send us word," she said quickly, before following the others to the bottom of the pool.

The Maestro sighed, as he began the walk back to Cadence Falls; if he was any judge, they were going to need all the help they could get!"

CHAPTER 11

Scales was having a marvellous time, flying high above the Ebunda River on his way to the Crescendo Range.

He wasn't allowed out on long journeys very often; only when he had things to transport, like the drums for the Fairy Festival or when he helped carry stuff for Landler and Polka's Handclasping Ceremony.

The Maestro had said to him: "It's not that we don't trust you, Scales, it's just that you're still young. We don't want you to overstretch your wing muscles, and remember, you <u>are</u> the only dragon we've got!"

Scales had said: "Yes, of course, Maestro," … but it was hard to watch his friends, Maeterlinck and Mahler, the bluebirds, fly the Maestro wherever he wished to go. (And they had to pull a carriage, too!)

And then there was Brand, Landler's favourite Beamer - they were <u>always</u> off on adventures. Brio, too! Even though he'd lost an eye, he <u>still</u> flew… behind Brand, who guided him.

But <u>then</u>… there had been Faye's rescue… they had actually needed <u>him</u> that time! He'd flown into the Cacophony Wood, <u>on his own</u> and had been the diversion that had allowed Landler and the Beamers to rescue, not only Faye, but <u>two</u> Inspiration Sprites! Everyone had fussed when they got back to Scores Hall, but the Maestro had been too pleased to have Faye and the Sprites safe again to be <u>really</u> angry with him.

Faye had sprung to his defence, too, which had resulted in the recently retired 'Timp' (Professor Timpani) taking him on as a student, so he could realise his dream of learning to play the drums!

However, there was one strange thing that had happened. For several days after this adventure, people kept asking him if he felt 'alright'. As the little dragon felt fine, he couldn't understand why this was, but one night he'd overheard the Maestro speaking to Fanfare in the little room next to his quarters. (He'd pretended to be asleep!)

"You're sure there's been no change in him, Fanfare?"

"None at all, Maestro. Scales is his usual happy self, and doesn't seem to have been affected by his time in the Cacophony Wood at all! It may well be that dragons are immune to the evil and sadness that lurk there!"

"I <u>wish</u> we knew for sure though, old friend; because he is the <u>only</u> dragon we have and, for that reason, I'm very reluctant to put Scales in any danger whatsoever!"

"Understood, of course… and yet, if he <u>could</u>…"

"Indeed!" The Maestro came out of the small room; Scales kept his breathing very even.

"Sleeping the sleep of the innocent," smiled Monody, glancing across at the little dragon… and he left.

Scales often thought about that conversation in the days to come… 'And yet, if he <u>could</u>…'

If he could what? Scales <u>wished</u> Fanfare had finished that sentence; he longed to know what it meant!

But now, suddenly, he was off on another adventure - the thought appealed to him.

He flew down to land in a small valley in the Range. He knew it was the right place, for he could see red glints in the rocks, which sparkled in the sun; Flame Rocks! Those were the ones he needed and he <u>now</u> knew exactly what to do with them!

Once the decision to send Scales had been made, Fanfare had gone to the Maestro's study and taken out the ancient books that his master kept in a secret drawer, known only to the two of them. Once Fanfare had read the relevant notes, he went to the identical drawer on the opposite side of the desk, and pushed a little carving of a butterfly, just under the keyhole.

Out sprang another secret compartment, only this time, instead of books, a purple velvet bag lay inside.

Fanfare took it out carefully and opened it: inside were an assortment of Flame Rocks, just the correct size to train a little dragon! The herald had no idea how long they had lain there, but now, if ever, was the right time to use them!

Fanfare went to collect Scales and they waited until everyone was at lunch, then they snuck into a corner of the courtyard for a quick first practice.

"Now, Scales," Fanfare began in his fussy way, "here are the Flame Rocks. You need to crush them by beating them with your tail, then scoop them into your mouth, swallow, and you <u>should</u> be able to produce Flame!"

Well, that sounded easy enough!

Scales did as he was told. He made quite a bit of noise, thumping his tail up and down and Fanfare glanced around nervously, but no one came out to investigate.

Next, came the scooping; Scales curled the claws of his forepaw over and had a good go, but the powdery substance kept falling through so, in desperation, he bent down, scooped it up with his tongue and swallowed.

He <u>really</u> wasn't prepared for how nasty it tasted! A cross between a <u>very</u> hot curry, soot, pondweed and an old pair of dirty socks! (Although Scales had tried neither curry nor socks, but you get the idea!)

Before Fanfare could stop him, Scales had dived on the nearest bucket of water and drank deeply… What happened next was inevitable.

A growling started low in Scales' stomach; it rose up to his throat, and as he opened it wide to belch, out his mouth shot a cloud of thick, black smoke that covered Fanfare from sight and brought several people running to the courtyard, shouting:

"Is there a fire? What's happened?"

The force of the expulsion had rocked the little dragon back on his heels and now he sat there, coughing and sneezing.

Fanfare, with great presence of mind, called out, "It's alright! I was just bringing some ashes out to dump them in the pit, when an ember flared up and set fire to the papers I was carrying. Scales saw, and quickly got a bucket of water to put the fire out! Sorry if we scared you!"

Everyone accepted this explanation easily and went back to their lunch.

"You'll have to practise in the Range," said Fanfare, wearily, "and remember… next time, <u>don't</u> drink water while you're doing it!"

Scales had remembered this, and <u>now,</u> he'd filled the three sacks the little herald had given him, and had done half an hours practice, by the end of which he could produce a respectable Flame!

He returned, happier than ever, to report back to Fanfare, and after <u>promising</u> that the <u>only</u> thing he would Flame at would be the Woodwind, Fanfare gave him the flight plan for his first mission.

It was short in distance, quick in time and easy. He was to fly Northwards, until he could spot the Woodwind in the distance, note which way it was travelling and report straight back!

As he took flight, the little dragon was so happy and excited that all the sadness in the world could not have dampened his spirits!

Three quarters of an hour into his mission, he saw it; a green, lazy snake-like could, meandering along in the distance. Scales made himself take a good, long look at it, so he'd recognise it again, took note of the direction in which it was heading, then turned to fly back to Scores Hall and report to Fanfare, who was anxiously awaiting him, (and secretly wishing that the Maestro was there, to take all of the problems onto his strong and wise shoulders.)

CHAPTER 12

The Warehouse, once just a place for storing barrels, winter supplies, hay and the occasional wheelbarrow, had now become a hive of activity. Row after row of assorted tables (everything from fine dining tables which were Fairy family heirlooms, to trestle tables that the Gnomes worked their craft on) were surrounded by the usual hotch-potch of chairs, stools and benches. Dash and Crumhorn had made a good job of organising the place, and Ocarina stood by the little stone-surrounded fire that they and Marcato had built that very morning (well away from the hay-store!) under a small skylight in the roof, which carried the smoke out by means of a long pipe.

A massive cooking pot was hung over the fire and, as Ocarina stirred, a lovely smell of stew began to drift out of the large doors, inviting everyone to supper.

People came in ones and twos at first, then more and more appeared until, at last, virtually the whole of Cadence Falls were seated around the tables, chatting animatedly.

Forlan had placed herself by the doorway, early on, to collect any more requests or reports for the Maestro, and although they had dealt with many earlier that day, she was still left clutching a sheaf of papers by the time everyone was in.

Forlana went to the small table that Dash had brought in from his own cottage, together with two beautiful dining chairs, (Presto's work; she knew at a glance.)

"This is for you and the Maestro," Dash had said. "Reckon you two 'ull want to talk about things private-like, with no one else buttin' in!"

"Thanks, Dash; that's really kind of you," she'd replied, and asked him to set them up not too far from the little curtained area where their mystery patient resided.

Forlana knew that the Maestro would want to keep an eye on him; added to which, they were far enough from the other tables to talk without being overheard.

She'd barely had time to sit down when, now, the Maestro came striding in.

Several people made as if to beckon him over, but with a wave and smile, he politely ignored their gestures, crossing to Forlana and plonking himself down on the opposite chair.

"Forlana, my dear. Thank you for saving me a seat… and <u>what</u> a seat! he said appreciatively, as he ran a finger over the fine carving. "Presto?"

"Dash, actually." She saw his surprised look, and continued, "oh, yes, <u>made</u> by Presto, of course, but provided for us by Dash, out of his own cottage."

"How very kind," said the Maestro, as Ocarina came up with two bowls of hot stew.

"Ah! Thank you, Ocarina. You don't need to wait on us, however."

"Nonsense!" replied Ocarina, briskly. "You two have far more important things to do. You just find a way to keep us all alive - we'll do everything else! Er… Maestro." She finished with a slight curtsey, as if she'd only just realised to whom she was speaking!

Monody chuckled. "We'll do our very best! By the way, has our patient woken up yet?"

"No, Maestro. I had Fretta check on him a little while ago. I think, though, that he's sleeping now, as opposed to unconscious, which is an improvement!"

"Good." The Maestro rose, looking down at his stew, wistfully, then went to the little platform that stood to one side. (It was normally used for hauling bales of hay up to the loft above.)

"My friends!" He projected his voice so that the place went quiet at once. "Now, don't stop eating," (several people had put down their spoons.) "We've all worked hard and we're all hungry! I just wanted to thank everyone for the immense effort you've all put in. So much has been achieved already!" He smiled at them all, glad to see how many tasks had been shared by Fairy and Gnome, alike. "Now that the Warehouse is ready, at the first sign of the Woodwind, <u>everyone</u> is to drop whatever they're doing and come here at once! We don't know how long it will linger, so we <u>must</u> have enough food and water to last several days. I'll go through all your reports tonight, then try and sort out what's needed. Thank you, my friends - now, relax and enjoy yourselves!"

There was a round of applause as Monody returned to his

seat… and his stew!

Forlana let him eat in peace before finally asking, in a quiet voice, "The new Olani?"

Monody gave her a small, sad smile.

"I chose correctly, which pleased the Council of Elders. I just wish it wasn't necessary."

Forlana nodded in sympathy.

The Maestro swallowed the lump in his throat.

"Celeste has been Olani since I was a youngling. She used to come to the surface and play with the others, back then. I know it's her time, but…"

"It's hard to let go, Maestro, but you wouldn't wish her to linger in pain."

"No, indeed I would not." He gave himself a little shake, then smiled at her, as three Gnomes started up a merry jig on fiddles and banjo.

"<u>That's</u> what we need! Play on boys!" The Maestro gestured to his people and several couples got up to dance.

Forlana looked at her master, questioningly.

"Is this the right time to be having a party?"

"It's <u>exactly</u> the right time! Don't you see, Forlana? Ever since we first heard of this wretched Woodwind, we've let it govern us! We've become worried, afraid, sad and serious… and that's before it <u>gets</u> here! We must remember, first and foremost, that we are <u>Music Fairies</u>! This is what we are created for! When did you last sing?"

"Not since we heard about…" she began.

"Exactly! Now, go and have some <u>fun</u>!"

He pulled Forlana out of her seat, then chuckled as Souza grabbed her hand and led her onto the floor.

The Maestro took the opportunity to skim quickly through the papers that Forlana had collected, while everyone was busy; some he could sort out with ease, but several of them were requests, asking him to find out if relatives were safe at Scores Hall or the Red Barn. Seeing as Monody very much wished to know this himself, he sighed as he put these papers in a separate pile.

Forlana returned, flustered and smiling, sat down and had a long drink of water.

"I don't know <u>where</u> Souza gets his energy from!" she laughed. "Ah! That's better… I love this song!"

After all the jigs and reels had finished, someone pushed Minima forward onto the platform and, once she'd had a quick word with the musicians, she began to sing an old Fairy folk-song. She had a beautiful mezzo-soprano voice, perfect for this melody, so everyone settled down to listen.

Minima had just started the second verse when the sound of an oboe joined the vocal line in a soulful harmony.

People began glancing around and Minima looked across at Monody, eyebrows raised, as if asking should she stop singing?

The Maestro rose and motioned to the singer to continue, everyone else to be quiet and, laying a hand on Forlana's shoulder, told her to stay where she was, as he went silently to the little curtained area and slowly peered round the edge…

The patient was awake!

Not only that, but he was sitting up, propped by the wall opposite. His eyes were shut and, as always, he was totally lost in his music.

One by one, the other musicians ceased to play; Minima, reducing her voice to a soft 'piano', was the last to finish… and then there was just the oboe.

Total silence resigned in the Warehouse - everyone recognising the fact that they were listening to a master of the instrument.

Eventually, the oboe solo came to a gentle and sustained end; the instrument was laid down reverently, the eyes opened and saw the Maestro coming forward gently, hands outstretched… and then, suddenly, there was a deafening noise!

Dirge shrank back into the corner, sheer panic in his face and Forlana, (who, out of curiosity, had come to see who was playing), was quickly dispatched by the Maestro to halt the thunderous applause and cheering which had erupted outside! As Forlana went to explain the problem, Monody turned back to the cowering figure and said, "I'm sorry if they startled you. They just wished to show appreciation for your beautiful performance. What is your name?"

"Dirge," came the reply.

"Do you know where you are?"

Dirge looked at the Maestro with pleading eyes.

"I… I hope I'm safe. Over the Barrier… where <u>she</u> can't get me! Am I? Am I safe?"

Monody nodded, with tears in his eyes.

"Have something to eat and drink; tomorrow we'll talk. You need to rest now."

The Maestro went out and beckoned Ocarina.

"Yes, Maestro?"

"Please can you bring some food and drink and that remedy of Fretta's to our patient in there?"

"Of course!"

He followed her across the room, then stopped in front of the tables and held a hand up for silence.

"Our injured friend is now awake, as you heard, but I think he has been through a terrible ordeal to get here, so I must ask for your patience... and restraint!" He grinned at two of the younger Gnomes who had been quietly strumming through the dance they intended to play next and they stopped, guiltily.

"Just for a couple of nights, lads, then we'll have all the music you can play!"

The two Gnomes smiled and nodded, then began to pack their instruments away.

That signaled the end of the evening and before long, Forlana and Monody were walking back, up the double hill towards Forlana's cottage.

"Maestro, did you learn any more from the patient, as to his identity?"

"Not <u>from</u> him, no," the Maestro replied, slowly, "but in all my time at Composition Magician, I've only ever known of <u>one</u> Fairy who can play the oboe that well."

He stopped and turned to Forlana.

"I think we've found Dale Van Clef!"

CHAPTER 13

The circular table in the secret chamber seemed somehow smaller and incomplete with the fifth chair standing empty. The four Fairies who had taken their places there, were all aware of it. Indeed, no one seemed to want to be the first to speak until, at length, the irascible Professor Cloche muttered, "Well, we can't all just sit here!"

"No! Of course not, I'm sorry." Fanfare coughed nervously and looked at each of them in turn. "It's just that…" he glanced at the empty seat next to him.

"Oh, do get on with it, Fanfare! the little Professor said, irritably. "Some of us have students to teach!"

"Indeed!" Now, the reason I asked you all to attend this meeting is to share some news with you."

Professor Tamburo looked down at his hands - he knew what was coming.

Fanfare took a deep breath.

"Scales has flown on a successful mission to discover in which direction this Woodwind is travelling."

Madame Leider and Professor Cloche looked at each other and then at Fanfare.

"Am I to understand," began the pompous portly Professor, "that you have taken it upon yourself to go against the Maestro's express wishes, the second his back is turned, and…"

Fanfare was growing paler by the second, when Tamburo came to his rescue.

"Now, now, Cloche, calm down. Poor Fanfare is doing the best he can in a very difficult situation. We need to know when and if the Woodwind will get here; the little dragon was very willing to go and has suffered no hurt at all! When Fanfare came to consult with me about the proposed trip…"

"What?? You knew about this? And you didn't see fit to inform me?"

"Or me, Professor Cloche!" Madame Leider's voice chimed in.

"You are not alone in being slighted," she continued, with the smallest of winks at Tamburo, "but since this… er… 'proposed trip' has already taken place, I suggest we listen to the outcome!"

Cloche spluttered a bit but quietened down enough for Fanfare to continue.

"Scales has discovered that the Woodwind is, at present, travelling in a North-Easterly direction, but if a crosswind springs up, this could change: we are in no <u>imminent</u> danger, but it <u>will</u> come this way, eventually!"

"What of Cadence Falls?" asked Madame Leider.

"And the Red Barn? If help is needed the solution is usually found there!" added Tamburo.

"I agree; we need to know if both places are safe. I have been monitoring the little dragon very carefully since his return, and I can assure you that he has had <u>no</u> ill effects at all!"

"But do you want to risk sending him out again, Fanfare? Supposing something happens to him - he is our <u>only</u> dragon, you know!"

"I'm well aware of that, Professor Cloche, but <u>he's</u> all we have at present. The bluebirds…"

"Oh of <u>course</u> you'd want to protect your precious bluebirds!"

Whatever reply Fanfare, drawing himself up in fury, was about to make, was drowned out by Madame Leider.

"ENOUGH!" She banged her fist on the table in a manner that would have made the Maestro very proud.

"We have a far more serious problem than who is flying where!"

The room went very quiet as Madame Leider drew a breath to continue.

"Professors Plagal and Symphonia came to see me this morning. They are very concerned about the Inspiration Sprites."

"Why?" Fanfare couldn't quite keep the panic out of his voice.

"Nothing to do with their safety, I do assure you."

His pleading look turned to one of relief.

"Well? What then?" Cloche snapped, testily.

Madame Leider turned to look at the professor, who gradually turned red and murmured, "I beg your pardon, Madame."

She inclined her head, then continued.

"Since the Maestro has been unable to return to Scores Hall, the Inspiration Sprites have not been sent into the Human world. We fear, if this continues to be the case, that it will result in a Deluge at Cadence Falls."

"The last thing we need is a Deluge!" said Tamburo. "Supposing it happened while the Woodwind was at Cadence Falls... They'd all die trying to clear it!"

As this was exactly what Fanfare had been thinking, he found it difficult to speak for a minute, but help came from an unexpected quarter. He found himself imagining not how the Maestro would respond to this, but what Forlana would say in the same situation.

Fanfare placed both hands on the table, sharply, and stood up.

"Right! That settles it. Scales will leave, as soon as possible for Cadence Falls, where he will pass on messages about the Deluge, the Woodwind, and anything else I feel is relevant. Scales will also be instructed to take note of the position of the Woodwind, during the journey, so that the Maestro might begin to plot its course. The dragon will then return to us with his report and any message the Maestro may wish to send. Thank you for coming. That is all."

Fanfare nodded briefly and left the chamber quickly and quietly, unaware of the astonished reaction of the three remaining Faires.

Indeed, he did not stop until he reached Scales' quarters, where he plonked himself down on a stool saying, "Oh my! Oh my!" over and over again, until Scales asked if he was alright.

"Um... yes... I think so. It's just that I've never... I mean... I wouldn't!"

He saw the little dragon's puzzled expression and forced himself to concentrate.

Upon being told that not only would he be flying to Cadence Falls, but possibly, (if the Maestro thought it wise) to the Red Barn, as well! Scales was so excited he could barely contain himself.

"No listen, Scales," Fanfare said, sternly. "This isn't a pleasure-trip, it's very important! You must look for the Woodwind, all the way to Cadence Falls and on the way back you will probably be carrying messages, which you must not lose! Do I make myself clear?"

"Yes. Yes, of course, Fanfare." The little dragon became serious all at once. "I wouldn't let you or the Maestro down; I know how important it is."

Fanfare looked at him, and knew he understood.

Relaxing a little, the herald crossed to a cupboard on the opposite wall and took out four sacks.

"Before you leave, you'll need to return to the Crescendo Range and fill these sacks with crushed Flame Rocks; that way, you'll have one sack to leave here, one to leave at Cadence Falls, and two spares to take wherever else you may need to go."

"Yes, Fanfare. I understand. I'm ready to go to the Range now, if that's alright?"

"Very well, Scales - off you go."

He watched the little dragon fly away towards the mountains, and only then allowed himself to indulge in a fit of the shakes, as he remembered how he had spoken to the illustrious member of the Circle of Five!

Scales, meanwhile, made good time to the Crescendo Range. This expedition took far less time than the first one had done, now Scales understood exactly how to crush the Flame Rocks. He positioned his tail so that the sharp spines along the edge did the hard work, rather than the soft part underneath, which hurt if he hit it too hard! Before long he had nearly filled all four sacks.

He was just crushing the last of the Flame Rocks he'd found, when he missed a swing and three of the rocks pinged out from under his tail and started to roll away down a little incline to his right. He dived and made a grab for them, dislodging several more pieces as he did so. Gathering the rocks in between his forepaws, Scales suddenly saw something glinting that <u>wasn't</u> red.

Puzzled, he bent down to the crevice in which it was lodged, for a closer look; it was the prettiest stone he had ever seen! He scooped it out and saw that delicate streaks of blue and purple ran through a strange, silvery, large, flat pebble, and the colours shimmered as he turned it this way and that.

Well, he wasn't about to crush <u>this</u> up! It was far too pretty. He'd take it back in one of the sacks and keep it in his quarters to look at.

Scales put it carefully away, and before long was flying steadily back to Scores Hall, carrying four full sacks.

***

On his return, he found everyone busy preparing for a possible siege. He couldn't see Fanfare as he flew down to land, so the little dragon put the four sacks in the corner of his quarters forgetting, in the buzz of activity, about the pretty stone he'd found.

Scales then settled down for a nap, (Fanfare always told him to eat or sleep after a flight) secure in the knowledge that the little herald would come and find him, when needed.

The little herald, meanwhile, had been drafted in to help organise the students, who showed an alarming tendency to regard a day off from their studies as a holiday.
Although everyone privately laughed at his fussy ways, the students knew that the Maestro trusted Fanfare as no other, so when <u>he</u> told them how important it was to get everything ready in case the Woodwind came, they didn't argue, but set to work with a will.

Miss Scrivens had been put in charge of a team to check all the storerooms to see what may prove useful, (much as Landler had done at the Red Barn) and just as Fanfare was about to check in on Scales, one of the Fairies on clean-up duty came running up to him, carrying a box.
"Ah, Fanfare, good! I've been looking for you; we've just found a box of fireworks in one of the storerooms. Miss Scrivens sent me to ask if you thought they'd be useful."
Fanfare peered into the box. Amongst the sparklers and Catherine wheels left over, no doubt, from when the circus came, there were several rockets.
Fanfare suddenly had an idea.
"Yes, thank you, Madrigal. Please would you be so kind as to put them in the Maestro's study, on his desk."
"Of course!" Madrigal sped off down the corridor with the box.
Fanfare made a quick round trip to see Madame Leider and Professor Cloche, (who was in a worse mood than usual, now that classes had been suspended) and finally Professor Tamburo.

On his last stop, Tamburo listened to his idea and said, "That's brilliant, Fanfare! Come on, let's do it now - I'll come with you!"
The two hurried to the Maestro's study and Fanfare, after looking through the rockets, chose a green one.
"Why green?" asked Tamburo.
"The Maestro had me going over many old records of human behaviour; he thinks it is important as we need the help of the humans in our world. One paper I read mentioned that humans use the colour red for 'danger' and green for 'all is well'. The Maestro knows this and will realise that, so far, Scores Hall is safe."
"Excellent! Where shall we set it from?"
"Well, I thought maybe the second room on the top floor. You know, the one where Madame Leider trains her soloists, so that no

one disturbs them? There is a small balcony - we could light it there."

"And no one will be there <u>now</u> as classes are cancelled. Let's go!" So saying, Professor Tamburo picked up a candle from the nearby windowsill and lit it.

The two of them went to the far end of the Hall, up one flight, then along the left-hand corridor and up the second.

They came to the room they needed, went in and unlocked the little door that led to the balcony.

The ledge around it was deep enough to stand the rocket on and after lighting the taper, both Fairies hurried back into the room, where they would be safe.

There was a whooshing noise as the rocket launched itself into the darkening sky. A couple of seconds went by and then a massive array of green stars shot out and danced across the blue velvet.

Fanfare turned to Tamburo.
"Let's hope he can see it!"

CHAPTER 14

Landler and Polka, together with Presto, Rollo and his team, sat wearily round a couple of tables, having a quick break from what had already been a long day's work.

Rollo and Presto had spent the whole day supervising at first, then joining in making the masks and oxy tanks everyone would need, eventually. There was now a respectable pile in the corner of the workshop, but Rolo was very much aware of the fact that, if they wished to protect their friends at Cadence Falls and Scores Hall, too, there wasn't nearly enough.

Polka, Viola and Felice had been working equally hard, distilling remedies and potions, so that they would be well stocked when the Woodwind came.

Landler had spent the afternoon in consultation with the Beamer Medics, making certain that they, too, had enough supplies and checking up on Brand and Brio who, though, improving, were still feeling the effects of inhaling the green mist and were certainly in no state to go on any more missions yet.

As Landler heaved a sigh, Polka turned from the food that Presto was offering her and said, "What's the matter, dearest?"

"I've been to see the Beamers, and there's no way <u>any</u> of them will be able to fly in the Woodwind."

"But Brand and Brio aren't in any danger, are they?" asked Presto, with a worried frown.

"No - they're improving, thankfully." Landler gave his friend a swift smile. "However, it doesn't solve the problem; we <u>still</u> can't communicate with the Maestro! We don't know where the Woodwind is - when it will reach us… or them! And I, for one, can't just sit here doing nothing!"

To no one's surprise, Landler sprang up and began pacing up and down.

Polka shook her head sadly at Presto.

"He's just exhausted; we <u>all</u> are! The Maestro will realise <u>why</u> we can't contact him, for the same reason that he can't get in touch with us! I wish…" she broke off, as a violent fit of coughing interrupted her.

Presto hastily poured out some water and gave it to her. Landler was by her side in an instant.

"Viola, when can Polka have some more of that concoction of yours?"

"Not yet, Landler; it's not that long since I gave her some."

"Well, it's not working, is it?!" He glared at Viola, who blinked, then he suddenly went to her and took her hand.

"I'm so sorry, Viola - that was unforgivable! It's just that she can't seem to shake it off!"

"I know, Landler." Viola patted his hand, "It'll just take a little time, that's all."

He nodded and smiled at her, then turned as Panno came racing in from outside.

"Landler! Quick! Come outside or you'll miss it!"

Landler and the others rushed outside and were just in time to see a cascade of green stars falling through the sky, then disappear. Lander whooped with joy then said to Panno, "Quick! The fireworks that Canto found, where are they?"

"In the small storeroom, I think."

"Bring them, and a torch, now!"

"Yes, Landler!" Panno dashed off, without knowing why.

Landler turned to the puzzled faces surrounding him.

"Scores Hall has sent us a signal!" he explained. "Green for 'all's well'! It means the Woodwind hasn't reached them yet - they're alright!"

A cheer went up; sheer relief on every face.

"What about Cadence Falls?" said Polka.

"We'll see. I'm going to send up a signal, too. If they see it at Cadence Falls, hopefully they'll do the same, if they can find any rockets."

Panno came running back with the box of fireworks; Canto carrying the torch (which he sensibly kept well away from the box.)

Landler rummaged through until he found what he was looking for.

"Here, Panno! Find something flat to stand these two on!"

Panno looked at the two rockets.

"Green… <u>and</u> blue?"

"Yes," Landler grinned, "Forlana will understand."

Polka nodded happily at him.

Two minutes later, the small party watched as the rockets exploded into the sky - blue and green mixing together.

Polka looked at Landler.

"Oh, I <u>hope</u> she sees them!"

***

"So what do you think happened to him, then?" Forlana asked, as she and the Maestro came to the top of the first hill on their way back to her cottage.

"I don't know, to be honest; he's obviously had a very bad injury to his leg and, judging by the scars, that must have happened some time ago." Monody paused for a second and frowned. "I can't be sure, of course, but I <u>think</u> he may have also sustained some sort of head injury, too, at some point - he seems very confused, but that could, of course, be due to the traumatic state he's in…"

A loud bang in the distance made them both turn round. A shower of green stars appeared to the West of them. The Maestro cheered.

"Look, Forlana! That's coming from the Hall! Green for 'all's well'! Good old Fanfare! He remembered the colour code the humans use… <u>and</u> he found fireworks!"

"Fireworks?"

"Yes! Do we have any here?"

"I'm not sure," Forlana thought for a moment. "Shawm would know - the Gnomes sometimes use them on special occasions."

"Let's go back to the Warehouse, then."

They set off, back down the hill again, but before long a second explosion, this time from the East, made them stop and gaze up at the sky.

"The Red Barn!" cried Forlana, triumphantly.

"Yes, indeed! Green… good, but green <u>and</u> blue? I don't know what to make of that?"

"I do!" cried Forlana. "Turquoise! That can only be from Landler! Turquoise is my favourite colour… he and Polka must be at the Red Barn… they're safe!"

She turned to the Maestro with happy tears in her eyes.

"Come on, Maestro! Let's go and find something to reply with!" She raced off down the hill, towards the crowd that had gathered outside the Warehouse soon after the first rocket had exploded.

The Maestro, chuckling at her headlong flight, followed her at a slightly slower pace. He was more relieved than he dared to admit that, for the moment, his friends and contemporaries at <u>both</u> locations were safe!

CHAPTER 15

"Now Scales, do I have your complete attention?"

"Yes, Fanfare."

"Because it is <u>very</u> important that you understand <u>everything</u> I say!"

"Yes, Fanfare."

"Now, you have the two sacks that I filled earlier from the Flame Rock you brought back?"

"Yes, Fanfare. You put them on me just now."

"<u>AND</u> the letter I have written to the Maestro? You mustn't lose it, that is <u>most</u> important!"

"Yes, Fanfare. It is in the topmost sack, where you put it... just now."

"Right! As soon as you arrive at Cadence Falls you will give the Maestro the letter and leave one of the sacks <u>there</u>. The other one is for your return journey home unless, of course, the Maestro decides to send you somewhere else... oh dear, should I make you take <u>three</u> sacks?"

"I think two will be enough," the little dragon replied, patiently. "I have just chewed quite a lot of Flame Rock, so that should last me some time - besides, we don't know if I'll even <u>see</u> the Woodwind on the journey."

The little herald sighed.

"True, true... Oh, alright, we'll stick to just the two sacks. Now then, the next thing is, <u>don't</u> overdo it."

"No, Fanfare."

"You <u>must</u> remember to eat and rest between each flight, so that you don't strain your wing muscles, and above all, you must be <u>very</u> careful not to inhale that green mist!"

"No Fanfare... I mean, yes, Fanfare, I will eat and rest, and no, I won't swallow the mist... <u>please</u> may I go now?"

Fanfare looked Scales up and down. The little dragon was obviously <u>so</u> excited to be chosen for the mission that not even the

Woodwind could dampen his spirits. Fanfare sighed.

"Just <u>one</u> more thing before you go, Scales. <u>Please</u> remember that you are the <u>only</u> dragon we have! You've <u>got</u> to come back in one piece!"

Scales looked at Fanfare and said, "I promise I'll come back! I'll be very careful, I'll remember <u>everything</u> you told me, and I <u>won't</u> let you or the Maestro down!"

With that, he turned and walked to the doors that led out of his quarters, crouched low, spread his wings and took off for Cadence Falls!

***

"You see, these are the keys - you push them down, like this, to make the different notes."

The Maestro nodded as 'Dirge' demonstrated and blew a lovely, rounded note from his oboe.

Monody had been trying, very gently, to find out a little more about his past, but made the mistake of saying, 'Is the person you are so afraid of, Dee Sharp?'

It took two strong Gnomes to hold him down and stop him from hurting himself. He cried out in terror, his eyes wild.

"No, no! Please don't let her find me! I can't go back! I'll do anything - PLEASE!"

Monody had spent twenty minutes talking quietly to the poor soul, telling him over and over again that he was safe and that no harm would come to him now he was with the Music Fairies.

Eventually he stopped thrashing and his breathing slowed.

The Maestro signaled Dal and Klang to leave, and once they'd gone he said, "So, tell me about your instrument; that's an oboe, isn't it?"

This was all that was needed to settle the patient once more.

'Dirge' picked up his beloved oboe and needed no encouragement to explain to Monody (who, of course, already knew) how it worked.

As the Maestro's aim was to calm him down so he could rest, once 'Dirge' had finished playing him a scale, the Maestro rose and said, "Thank you for showing me, Dirge; that was really interesting, but, I'm afraid I must leave you to rest now, of Fretta will tell me off for tiring you too much!"

'Dirge' smiled at him and said, "I like talking to you - will you come again?"

"Of course." He patted the hand that clutched the oboe. (They had learnt not to take it from him while he slept, as he grew very panicky without it.)

"Try and get some rest now."

"I will, M… Maestro?"

"That's right," Monody smiled at him, and left through the curtains, where his smile faded a little, as he'd hoped the use of his title might jog the patient's memory… but so far, it hadn't.

Forlana, who had been waiting impatiently outside, practically leaped at her master.

"Well, have you found out what Dee Sharp's plan is, Maestro?"

"No, not yet. I'm afraid we are a long way from learning anything soon… It is my fear that that poor soul has lived amongst darkness and decay for so long that it may have damaged his brain, permanently! We need to proceed slowly and carefully with him."

Forlana was unimpressed.

"But we need that information <u>now</u>, Maestro! Can't you <u>make</u> him tell us?"

The second she said it, Forlana realised she'd gone too far. There was a moment's silence, then the Maestro raised his head slowly, and looked at her. His expression made her blush to the roots of her hair as she hung her head in shame.

"Forlana," the Maestro began, very quietly, "if this is <u>indeed</u> Dale Van Clef, can you not see that we have to be very gentle with him if he's to have <u>any</u> sort of a normal life again. I would also remind you that Dale was a Crystal Seeker, without whom, the Music Fairies would <u>not</u> survive!"

"I'm so sorry, Maestro," Forlana said, in a small voice. "I don't know what came over me… it's just that… when I can <u>do</u> something, I'm fine, but when it comes to sitting around, waiting…"

"You forget, my dear," the Maestro gave her a little smile of forgiveness, "I've known you a long time! But please, just try to be…"

"<u>DRAGON!</u>"

They both turned towards the large doors and saw Glock pelting in, and skidding to a halt in front of them.

"Dragon? Do you mean Scales?"

Glock nodded. Having run up and down <u>both</u> hills, he was close to collapse!

"Come on, Maestro!"

Forlana almost pushed Monody out the door, so anxious was she to see if there was news.

They both looked up and could just make out the little dragon in the distance. Forlana undid the turquoise sash she wore and began to wave it above her head.

After a few moments, Scales changed direction slightly and proceeded to veer towards them.

"He's seen us, Maestro!"

"indeed, he has."

Forlana frowned at the lack of enthusiasm in her master's voice, then she realised - he was worried that the little dragon may have over-stretched himself.

However, as Scales made his descent, his excited chatter made Monody laugh.

"Maestro! Forlana! It's <u>so</u> good to see you. I flew <u>all</u> the way here <u>and</u> I didn't get lost… Fanfare <u>will</u> be surprised!"

As he touched down, Forlana ran to give him a hug, which was so unlike her that both the dragon and Monody looked at each other in surprise. Scales then took a step forward and bowed to his master.

"Maestro, there is a letter for you from Fanfare. It is in the topmost sack and Fanfare asks you to read it at once."

(He spoke as if he were reciting a poem, having learnt the words by heart.)

"Thank you, Scales. I shall read it presently, but first of all, I would like Mallika to check you over, just to make sure you haven't strained any wing muscles."

The little dragon looked as though he was about to sigh, but one look at Forlana's face made him think better of it, and said, "Of course, Maestro," as Forlana pulled his head down so she could detach the two sacks from round his neck.

Catch and Glee were just returning to the Warehouse, so Forlana grabbed them.

"Could you two take a sack each, please. Store them inside - <u>nowhere</u> near the cooking area; Flame Rock!" she added, having peeked inside when she took out Fanfare's letter.

"Right, Forlana." The two Gomes hefted a sack each onto their shoulders and went inside.

"Fretta!" Monody called to the Fairy who was just by the door. "Please could you take Scales and get him checked by Mallika."

"Of course, Maestro."

She led Scales off, while Monody and Forlana went to their table where, after a sip of Lupin tea, which Minima had left ready for them, Monody opened and read the letter while Forlana studied his face.

She saw from his expression that there was bad news and waited, with a sinking heart, for him to finish.

At length, he put the letter down, looked up at Forlana and said, "Two of the Inspiration Sprites are sick, and Fanfare is worried that, if the Sprites can't be sent out to the human composers, (which they can't, of course; it's much too dangerous!) we'll have a Deluge soon to deal with, as well as the Woodwind!"

Forlana gasped, putting her hand to her mouth.

"But, Maestro, if there's a Deluge while the Woodwind is here, we won't be able to get outside to deal with it!"

"Exactly. Without the Music Fairies containing the angry Dots, they will all be drawn to Dee Sharp's castle and turned into more Discords. She will then have everything she needs to destroy us - once and for all."

For once in her life, Forlana could think of nothing to say, but the look she gave her master said it all.

He rose and went to her, patting her shoulder with one hand, whilst laying the letter in front of her with the other.

"Excuse me for a moment, my dear, I must speak to Scales."

She nodded, the letter in hand, and the Maestro went to the far side of the Warehouse, where Mallika had just finished her examination.

"You've done very well, Scales," she was saying as Monody joined them, "no damage at all, as far as I can see!" She patted the little dragon's nose.

"Thank you, Mallika."

"Oh, Maestro!" She turned to him. "He looks absolutely fine to me,"

"Good." Monody smiled at her. "Will he be fit to fly again… tomorrow?"

"I see no reason why not; he's young, strong and healthy."

"Scales," Monody turned to face him. "After you've had a good rest tonight, do you think you would be able to take me back to Scores Hall tomorrow, or would that be too much for you?"

"I'd be happy to, Maestro! And Fanfare would be <u>very</u> happy to see you, too!" Scales couldn't believe his luck, he was delighted to be of so much use and to the Maestro, of all people!

"There's just one thing…" he said, before he could stop himself.

"Yes?"

"I'm <u>very</u> hungry," the little dragon sighed, wistfully.

Monody laughed and patted him.

"Well, that's easily fixed." He turned to Mallika, who was already on her way.

"Leave it to me, Maestro! I'll get a couple of buckets of scraps organised… <u>and</u> one of water!" she added, as she saw the Maestro about to ask.

That sorted, Monody went to find Shawm.

By the time Forlana came to join them, having read the letter, the Maestro was just about to find her.

"Ah, forlana, perfect timing! I've just been telling Shawm that I must return to Scores Hall tomorrow."

Forlana tried not to show the sudden panic she felt.

"I'm leaving you in charge."

(The panic rose to her throat.)

"With Shawm, here, as your second. Between the two of you, you should be able to take care of things until I can get back."

"Oh, you <u>are</u> coming back?" she couldn't keep the relief out of her voice.

"Yes, eventually, but there are several things I must do, first."

Forlana drew a deep breath, then nodded.

"I'm sure Shawm and I can cope in your absence, Maestro."

"I <u>know</u> you can."

The rest of the afternoon was spent in compiling lists and taking down instructions from Monody as to what else needed doing, together with Shawm. In fact, they'd been so busy that all three were surprised when they finally finished, to see that it was dark, and people were gathering in the Warehouse for the evening meal.

The Maestro glanced over to the far corner, Scales having eaten a huge meal, was now curled up, fast asleep.

They too, proceeded to eat a hearty meal and then, as had become the custom, they all came together for an evening of music, which lifted everyone's spirits.

Forlana noticed that 'Dirge/Dale' hovered on the edge of the curtains now to play, almost in the room, but not quite. Well, that was progress!

Monody leaned across to her, under the cover of the music and said, "I know you would rather be with Landler and Polka, but the fact is, my dear, I need you <u>here</u>!"

"Thank you, Maestro. I'll do my best here, but if you happen to see Landler, tell him I understood the two rockets."

The Maestro nodded, as they both watched the enjoyment of their musical friends, both determined to protect them <u>and</u> their way of life!

CHAPTER 16

"Yes, but _how_?" Landler did his level best to keep the frustration out of his voice, as he knew he'd been snapping and irritable with everyone all day.

They had _all_ worked hard, and now had several dozen masks and oxytanks, waiting to be delivered. But with no means of transporting them, they just sat in a corner of the barn, gathering dust, as Polka had put it.

They had reluctantly decided that there wouldn't be enough to supply Galliard and Bagatelle but, as the Woodwind had already hit, Landler could only hope that it had blown past them now, leaving those who _hadn't_ been caught out in it to cope as best they could!

Presto, Rollo and Polka sat around the table and, as no one had an answer for Landler, they remained silent; except for Polka who, every so often, had a slight fit of coughing. Landler glanced across at her, but she gave him a weary wave, so he had to be content with that as, between the four of them, they were virtually running everything at the Red Barn.

They'd worked late over the past few days and Polka, although still her usual cheery self, was looking pale and tired, and had even lost a little weight. Landler was the first to notice that she seemed to have no appetite and even though she'd been helping out in the kitchens (when she wasn't busy distilling potions and remedies), she hadn't had _one_ of her usual baking frenzies!

Landler reached over and patted her hand.

"Why don't you go and have a long soak in one of the shell baths, then go to bed?"

Polka nodded wearily, smiled at the others, then left.

Rollo, Presto and Landler then discussed their limited options.

"So… at the moment," concluded Landler, "what we know, so far, is that all appear to be safe at both Scores Hall and Cadence Falls, but for how long? They _need_ those masks!"

"Well, the Beamers certainly can't fly in the Woodwind - they've already proved that!" said Presto, with concern.

Although out of danger, Brand and Brio were still recovering from the effects of inhaling the green mist, when they went to rescue Landler and Polka from Pavane Villa, four days earlier. The Beamer Medics had advised against sending <u>any</u> of them out after that and, as they had been friends since they were younglings, and though he <u>knew</u> Brand would fly him anywhere, anytime, Landler wouldn't risk him.

He looked at Rollo for a solution but when he, too, sighed and shook his head, Landler stood up.

"No point beating our brains over it anymore tonight; we're all too tired to think straight. Come on, let's get some sleep and begin fresh tomorrow."

Rollo and Presto nodded, then walked with Landler out of the main hall towards the sleeping quarters.

***

Scales beat his wings steady and strong, proud to be flying his master back to Scores Hall. Everyone would see them arrive and know who was returning their Maestro to them!

Monody meanwhile, was noticing with approval that the little dragon's wing muscles looked to be in good working order, as he flew steadily without tiring. This thought pleased him for a moment, but then his brain flipped straight back to all the worries that beset him.

<u>So far</u>, it appeared that the folk at the Red Barn and Scores Hall were safe, but he still felt for those at the villages lying to the North-West, Galliard and Bagatelle; no one had heard anything from them since the final robin message, a few days ago.

Then again, Monody was itching to go to the Red Barn to see if Rollo and Presto had come up with anything which might help them, but he knew it was his duty to be at Scores Hall; the centre of music in Octavia, where he would be able to do the most good for his people.

He sighed again - 'his people', his special team of people whom he had trained and needed <u>with</u> him, now, were dotted about all over the place, with no means of communication <u>or</u> transport... which brought him back to Scales!

It was plain to see that the little dragon hadn't been affected at all by the Woodwind... another twenty or so, and <u>that</u> particular problem would be solved.

<u>Why</u> was Scales the only dragon? That question had puzzled everyone since the day, long ago, when they'd woken up to find all the dragons of the Crescendo Range had disappeared... all except one little egg!

Monody shook his head to clear it as they turned to meet the Ebunda River, which they would follow down to the Hall, when, to his horror, he saw the swirling green mist not too far behind!

The wind had picked up and, as the Maestro glanced back over his shoulder, it seemed as though the Woodwind had seen him, and was giving chase!

He knew Scales had seen it, too, for the little dragon suddenly redoubled his efforts and sped ever homewards.

The second they reached the courtyard Monody yelled to Scales, "Well done, my friend! Now go to your quarters, eat and rest, then someone will come through the tunnels with instructions for you!"

"Yes, Maestro, thank you!"

With a little bow, Scales flew off to his quarters, situated round the back of the Hall.

Monody then went to a couple of Fairies who were crossing the courtyard and asked one to go to the kitchens to find food and water for Scales, and the other to find Fanfare and send him, with all haste, to the master's study...

"Then ask Tanto to sound the Alpen Horn, as the Woodwind is coming!"

The Fairies raced to do his bidding, while Monody strode quickly to his study. He was pleased he didn't have to waste time searching for the box of fireworks, for there it was, on his desk!

He selected a red rocket, took a candle from the mantelpiece then, with long strides, headed for the stairs at the end of the corridor. As he started up, a small figure came racing to meet him.

"Maestro! Thank goodness!" Fanfare couldn't quite manage to keep the relief out of his voice.

The Maestro looked at him and managed a small smile.

"My friend... it's coming!"

Fanfare grew pale.

"I need you to gather the Circle immediately - I will join you as soon as I've lit this!"

"At once, Maestro. The balcony room!" he called back as he dashed off and Monody, with his long legs, made short work of the climb to the top floor where, not so long ago, Fanfare had confidently lit the green rocket for 'all's well' that he and Forlana had seen from Cadence Falls.

Quickly he lit the taper and stepped back from the balcony.

The rocket shot up and red stars exploded everywhere. He only watched it for a second, then shut the balcony doors firmly, but not before he'd seen the Woodwind, to his right, swirling ever nearer.

People in the courtyard ran, but not in panic for, ever since the Cacophony Wood and Dee Sharp's castle had appeared, he'd drilled the Music Fairies as to what to do in an emergency, only he'd always thought the danger would come in the shape of a battle... not this invidious mist!

Suddenly, a loud klaxon rang out - Tanto on the Alpen Horn.

Monody took that as his signal to join the Circle of Five, who would all be waiting for a rescue plan which, so far, the Maestro didn't have!

CHAPTER 17

A lone figure was slowly making its way through the Cacophony Wood. It staggered from tree to tree, touching the dead trunks with virtually no ill effect, until at last it collapsed, exhausted, leaning against a trunk for support.

Dee Sharp looked at her surroundings. She had never been this far away from the castle before, as Dirge always went outside; if needed.

However, she'd run out of supplies she'd found in and around the kitchen, so now she'd been forced to go on a search for something - <u>anything</u> to eat!

For though the enchantress had copied out many magic spells, she'd never bothered with anything that wasn't evil; consequently, she didn't have one spell that would have provided her with a much-needed dinner!

(Even more ironically, all her spells were kept safe in the back of... a cookbook, which she didn't know how to use!)

On the journey, she'd managed to find a few berries and mushrooms which still grew, somehow, in the dark wood, but the berries had made her violently ill, so she didn't dare try <u>them</u> again! The mushrooms and some water in an old, cracked jug she'd found had been her sole nourishment now for three days! Only her rage over Dirge's desertion kept her going.

Two of her guards had accompanied her at the start of her journey, but the farther they got from the castle, the weaker they had become.

As she looked at them, first one, then the other started to fade; until they were virtually transparent. Dee Sharp wondered bitterly if the ones at the castle were disappearing, too! It was her best-kept secret that <u>none</u> of her creations (apart from the Woodwind) could cross the Bar Barrier; she wasn't even sure if Dirge knew this, or not.

Dirge... she <u>couldn't</u> work out why he had left.

At first, she had glanced around the wood as she went, searching for him, but soon stopped herself.

She couldn't afford to start caring at this point; her only aim <u>now</u> was to reach the Bar Barrier and, with the power of the Woodwind behind her, attempt to cross and destroy the Music Fairies (and Dirge, too… if he got in her way!) at the source.

Hatred drove her on!

***

Forlana sat under her favourite cherry tree on the little green, at the end of her first day as leader, after the Maestro had left on Scales and laughed ruefully at herself.

Some leader <u>she'd</u> turned out to be!

Monody had barely gone before they'd had a small fire, (because Fling had accidentally left a bale of straw near the open fire, instead of moving it down the other end!) It had caught light, and only Dash and Crumhorn's quick action with buckets of water had stopped it burning the whole Warehouse to the ground!

After a short, sharp and <u>very</u> loud lecture on fire hazards, Forlana had spent the entire afternoon swamped in paperwork, organising more foraging teams, either for food, or herbs and plants, and then, just as they were settling down to the evening meal, <u>another</u> disturbance had occurred!

All the tasks were shared out equally, and it just so happened that Crumhorn had been selected to take the 'patient' his food. What happened next was inevitable for, as soon as Crumhorn clapped his eyes on 'Dirge' he dropped the tray with a loud clatter and ran, yelling for Sackbut to flee.

Lilt and Dash had raced to their Goblin friends and tried to calm them down. (Sackbut was panicking too, by now, although he had no idea what about!)

Meanwhile, Forlana and Fretta ran to see 'Dirge/Dale' who was cowering in the corner of his bed, unsure what had just happened, but afraid, nevertheless!

Forlana, brilliant in any crisis that called for organisation, bravery and action, looked helplessly at Fretta, who was trying to collect all the broken crockery from around the floor.

"Go on, Forlana!" whispered Fretta, shooing her towards Dirge. "You deal with him, while I sort this lot out. I'll bring more food, presently."

"Couldn't <u>I</u> do that?" Forlana asked, pleadingly.

Fretta shook her head.

"<u>You're</u> in charge!"

Forlana heaved a sigh, then went to sit on the edge of the bed, patting Dirge's shoulder awkwardly, saying, "There, there, everything's alright," with a lot more conviction than she felt. She <u>wished</u> Polka was there - she always knew what to do in these situations!

Almost without realising it, she began to borrow phrases from the plump Fairies vocabulary, imitating her soft tones.

"Now, Dirge, is it? Listen to me, the... er... Gnome who brought your food in just now, was once a prisoner of Dee Sharps..."

He immediately raised terrified eyes to hers. Biting back a sigh, she made herself continue, calmly.

"No, no, it's alright - she's not here. But Crumhorn was afraid if you saw him, you'd make him go back to her castle. He was afraid of <u>you</u>, do you see?"

"Afraid... of <u>me</u>? But I'm afraid of her, too! I'd <u>never</u> want anyone to have to live in that castle!" he shuddered.

"That's good then, Dirge, I'll tell him that, then he won't be scared any more. Look! Here's Fretta with some more food for you. Come now, eat. You want to get well, don't you?"

Dirge nodded and accepted Fretta's tray.

Both Fairies watched him pick up the spoon, then they left him to it.

Forlana went to the table where Lilt and Dash were hovering protectively over the two Goblins.

"We won't let 'im take 'em back, Forlana," said Dash, coming up to face her.

"No one's taking anybody!" she said, with as much patience as she could muster (which was <u>very</u> little, by now!) but she forced herself to sit down and explain, quietly, that Dirge was every bit as scared of being sent back as they were!

Doubt gave way to incredulous relief, and such was Forlana's success with them that, when she suggested, after the meal, that they go with her and talk to Dirge properly, they agreed… much to her surprise!

The meeting, after a very edgy start, went better than anyone could have expected and, once the Goblins realised that Dirge had lost his memory and had no recollection of them at all, they relaxed and began to chat about normal things, chiefly how good the food was here, and by the time Sackbut had related the tale of his first experience with 'Whoops-A-Daisy' beer, Dirge was even smiling!

"Well handled, Forlana," said Fretta, quietly, as the two Fairies moved away, leaving the trio to chat.

"Thanks!" Forlana sighed with relief.

That had been an hour ago, and now, as she perched under the softly-glowing cherry tree, Forlana thought to herself: 'Well, if that's what being a leader is all about, the Maestro is welcome to it!'

CHAPTER 18

In the secret chamber, four out of the five Fairies sat in varying stages of agitation.

Fanfare was flustered, having been asked by the Maestro to remain with the Circle, until Landler could return. Madame Leider sat with her hands clutched tensely in her lap, looking down at them. Tamburo leaned his head on his fist and frowned; and, finally, Professor Cloche kept looking at his time piece and tutting.

Monody glanced at each one in turn, reading their expressions, trying to gauge what their reactions would be… So far, he had formed only a very small part of the plan, but he was hoping, once the first piece was in place, that inspiration would come, as to the next!

He drew a deep breath and four pairs of eyes immediately fixed on his.

"Thank you for coming at such short notice." A mutter of 'students' and 'classes' came from Cloche's direction, but he ignored it.

"I watched Scales very carefully as we flew back here, and I'm pleased to report that he can fly exceptionally well; he is delighted to be of use, and the Woodwind seems to have absolutely no effect on him whatsoever!"

"But Maestro, what will happen if we keep sending him out?" said Madame Leider, worriedly.

"That is something I do not, as yet know… which is why I shall only send him on essential journeys. I wish the other dragons had not left; we need them now as ever before because, if this immunity is a draconic trait, they would be invaluable to us!"

He sighed.

Tamburo looked up. "It must have been an illness, Maestro! No other reason could have caused the dragons to leave - they loved it in the Crescendo Range… it was their home!"

"And no female dragon would willingly leave an egg behind!" put in Madame Leider.

She was referring to Scales, of course, because when no sound had been heard from the dragons, a team was sent out to investigate. They found no trace of the dragons, (which ruled out illness in the Maestro's opinion) but one of the team suddenly heard a sound coming from a small cliff below. She peered over and there, crying piteously, was a newly-hatched dragonet. They knew it wouldn't survive on its own, so the team clambered down to rescue it and took it back to Scores Hall, where Fanfare and Monody had reared it between them... so it was understandable that Fanfare, with real concern in his eyes, said quietly, "We can't lose him, Maestro."

"I don't intend to!" Monody whispered, then was interrupted by the irascible Cloche.

"Yes, yes, this is all very well, but it doesn't help us <u>now</u>! YOU'RE the Composition Magician; can't <u>you</u> call them back?"

He actually jabbed a finger at Monody, but the reaction of the other three quickly made him withdraw it.

The Maestro looked directly at him.
"Believe me, Professor, I would, if it were possible; However, <u>as you know,</u> (he stressed each word) the Draconic Stone went missing at the same time as the dragons disappeared, and without it, I cannot even discover if there is <u>one</u> other dragon in the vicinity!"

Cloche went very red and sat in sulky silence.

Fanfare very privately wished there was a way to get him off the Circle - he never seemed to contribute anything positive, and spent all his time trying to anger the rest of the Circle, as far as <u>he</u> could see!

The Maestro continued smoothly. "So, let us concern ourselves with what we <u>can</u> do: I propose that we send Scales out tomorrow to the Red Barn, to collect however many masks Rollo and his excellent team have been able to make. After suitable rest, Scales will then fly to Cadence Falls, deliver their masks and oxytanks, then return to us with whatever is left, for <u>our</u> use."

"Oh, yes, of course! We're last - <u>we</u> get the leftovers!"

Tamburo stood up and banged his fist on the table, perilously close to Cloche's hand, which he snatched away, just in time!

"Cloche... if you can't say anything useful... <u>go away</u>!" He didn't shout, but spoke quietly through clenched teeth which, somehow, was much more scary.

Cloche took one look at Taburo's blazing eyes and, with more haste than dignity, fled the room.

Tamburp's check was heaving, but he turned to Monody and

bowed.

"I must beg pardon, Maestro, but really, the way he speaks to you!"

"Thank you, Tamburo." The Maestro nodded and the professor sat back down.

"Now, back to business; all in favour of Scales going to get the masks?"

Everyone round the table agreed.

"Good. I shall send a message to that effect, which brings me to the next problem we must discuss…"

But what that was, they didn't discover for, just then, the outer study door was flung open with some force. Monody put a finger to his lips and they all remained silent.

They heard shouts of "No! He's not in here - where can he be?"

The door slammed shut once more.

Monody signaled Fanfare to go and see if the coast was clear; he disappeared for a minute, then came back and nodded.

Monody stood up. "It appears I am needed. Thank you for coming: if anything else requires discussion, I'll inform you."

"Maestro," Madame Leider laid her hand on his arm as she left, "we trust you; whatever <u>you</u> think is the right thing to do, we're behind you."

"Thank you, my dear."

He saw Tamburo out, then closed the door to the secret chamber behind him. Fanfare let them leave the study, one at a time, in case anyone saw them, then he and Monody shut the study door and headed towards the Maestro's own study.

They hadn't got far before they saw Melodia and Plagal racing to meet them.

"Maestro, thank goodness! We've been looking for you everywhere!" cried Melodia. Before he had a chance to reply, Plagal broke in.

"Maestro, <u>please</u>… we have eight Fairies who were caught out in the mist… two of them are really sick. I'm afraid… please, come <u>now</u>, Maestro!" Plagal was close to tears.

"I'm coming, Plagal. Just let me get some Vivace Drops from the study."

"Thank you!"

The two Fairies ran off, back towards the infirmary.

Monody turned to Fanfare, with deep sorrow in his eyes.

"And so… it begins."

CHAPTER 19

Another burst of controlled flame seared away a patch of green as Scales watched it shrivel with satisfaction.

He flew steadily, taking note of exactly where he was each time he created a gap in the Woodwind. He was surrounded by it and yet, it didn't bother him one bit.

Being of a naturally sunny disposition, the evil and sadness that dwelt in the mist, and was so dangerous to the Fairy folk, didn't affect him at all!

Besides, he was simply overjoyed to be able to see all of his friends and help them. He <u>must</u> remember to tell Landler that the Woodwind had reached Scores Hall! That was one of the many instructions that Fanfare had given him earlier. He had come through the tunnel that led to the Magical Creatures section of the Hall to inform Scales of the Maestro's decision.

"However," Fanfare added, "the Woodwind is now all around us, and, if you are willing to go to the Red Barn, you will have to fly through it!"

"The Red Barn?" Scales cried excitedly. "When can I leave? Now?"

"No!" Fanfare replied firmly. "Did you understand about the Woodwind?"

"Yes, Fanfare - I fly through and then flame it out of the way, so I can see!"

Fanfare looked at the little dragon. It was obvious that the thought of all that sickly, green mist really didn't phase him in the least, (whereas it made Fanfare feel ill every time he thought of it!) With a sigh, Fanfare continued, "Have you eaten?"

"Yes, Fanfare."

"Have you rested?"

"Yes, Fanfare."

There was absolutely no reason not to let him go.

"And your Flame Rock sacks full?"

"Yes, Fanfare."

"Do you have the letter the Maestro wrote to Landler?"

"Yes, Fanfare."

"Remember to fly straight there, tell Landler the Woodwind is here; give him the letter, and ask Rollo for all the masks and oxy-tanks they have. Then EAT and REST before you go to Cadence Falls to deliver them!"

"Yes, Fanfare. And then I eat and rest again before I bring any spare masks back here."

He really <u>did</u> understand, Fanfare thought and, very uncharacteristically for him, went to pat the little dragon affectionately on the nose.

"Just come back safe, please."

"I will, Fanfare, I promise... Please can I go now?"

"Yes Scales, you can go."

And, finally, he was on his way to help his friends.

It wasn't too long before he cleared the Woodwind and was able to fly without hindrance to the Red Barn, where fortunately, the green mist hadn't yet arrived.

As he executed a perfect landing just outside the main barn, Landler, (who had been visiting Brand and Brio in the Medics wing) turned the corner and let out a great whoop of joy as he saw the little dragon.

"Scales! By all that's wonderful! We've been racking our brains to think of a way..."

"... to deliver the masks... I know! That's why I'm here!" Scales finished for him.

It was hard to know who was more excited for a few seconds, as Landler jumped about, thumping Scales on the foreleg, and the little dragon trumpeting with glee, which nearly shook every building in the place!

It was no surprise then that many folk, alerted by the racket, ran out to see what was happening, Polka being one of them.

"Scales! How lovely to see you! But, should you have come? I mean, the Woodwind, it's dangerous!"

"Oh, that's alright!" the little dragon said blithely, "I've already flown through it!"

This had the effect of completely silencing everyone in mid-cheer.

"Where?" Polka asked, faintly.

"At Scores Hall," he replied. "Landler, Fanfare said I was to tell you it has arrived, if you didn't already know."

Landler nodded. "I wasn't sure..."

He looked guiltily at Polka, whose eyes were wide.

"I saw the red rocket explode, but didn't want to panic everyone until I was certain."

The Fairy fold looked at each other, trying to absorb the news.

"So, it'll be here soon?" That was Rollo, who had come out to see where half his workforce had disappeared to.

"Yes, I think so," Scales said, honestly. "It's quite difficult to tell, because the direction of the wind keeps changing but, yes, sometime soon."

"Right, then! Let's get Scales loaded up, now!" Landler sprang into action, but Polka's 'Wait!' stopped him mid-stride.

"Scales," she turned to face him. "What other instructions did Fanfare give you?"

The little dragon half-closed his eyes in concentration.

"Go to the Red Barn. Tell Landler about the Woodwind. Give him the Maestro's letter, and… ask them to get all the masks ready, oh! And eat and rest before I fly to Cadence Falls to deliver them!"

He looked up, pleased he'd remembered it all, but Polka had turned to Landler and said, "There! I thought so! He's to eat and rest before he goes anywhere!"

"But, Polka!…"

"He's the only dragon," she said sternly.

Landler frowned for a minute then said, "Very well, somebody get him some food!" before he stalked off into the Barn.

Scales watched him go, in concern.

"Have I made Landler angry? I'm sorry. I could leave now, only Fanfare said…"

"Fanfare has sense, which is more than I can say for some people."

Scales was puzzled; he'd never heard Polka sound really cross before - Polka was always happy!

Presto came up to them.

"It's alright, Scales. Landler's not angry with you, he's just impatient, that's all. Come on, I think I can see your food arriving!"

Four strong Fairies were lugging huge buckets of food out to the courtyard, followed by another two dragging a big metal container full of water.

"There you go! Eat as much as you want, then have a good sleep, and, Scales…"

Yes, Presto?"

"Thank you for coming."

Landler reappeared later, somewhat calmer since reading the

Maestro's letter, and went to find Polka. She was in the Distillery and, when she turned to face him, she gave him a smile which didn't quite reach her eyes.

"I've read the Maestro's letter," he began, leading her to a stool and sitting opposite her. "He wishes me to go on Scales tomorrow, after we've <u>both</u> eaten and rested…" he laughed ruefully, "… to show the folks at Cadence Falls how to use the masks and oxy-tanks, and then… I'm to return to Scores Hall."

He waited to see how she would take the news.

"Of course you must go… if the Maestro wishes it," she said quietly, not looking at him.

"It's orders, dearest, I don't <u>want</u> to leave you, but I must."

"I'll be fine," she replied, but then broke off for yet another coughing fit.

He watched her, worriedly, until it passed.

"I'm needed here, anyway; if folks get sick, I can tend to them."

"And look after yourself!" he said with concern.

"Of course, Landler," she replied without enthusiasm, and she didn't call him dearest as she would normally have done.

Landler sighed; when this was over, he'd make it all up to her, but for now, he had to do his duty!

CHAPTER 20

Landler was surprised, but pleased to discover, the following morning, that Presto was going, too!

"Rollo says he can spare me now, so I'll come with you and stay at Cadence Falls to tell folks about the masks, which means <u>you</u> can then go to the Maestro, see what he needs doing then get back to Polka! I know you're not happy about leaving her."

Landler stopped strapping on the storage kits to Scales and looked at his friend.

"It's not just the coughing… she… she's <u>different</u> somehow."

"I wouldn't worry too much, Landler. We're <u>all</u> exhausted and under pressure. She's probably irritable because she's tired."

Landler gave him a swift smile as they finished loading Scales up with masks and oxy-tanks, but he knew his Polka, and <u>something</u> wasn't right!

When they stepped back to check their handiwork, Presto suddenly said, "I say, Scales, it won't be too much for you to carry me as well, will it?"

Scales looked at Presto's slim, lean shape and replied, "No, Presto. Not at all."

"I'll just get my backpack then, Landler."

Landler followed him into the Barn and found Polka waiting for him.

"Presto's coming with me, so that I can return to you more quickly."

"That's kind of him, but I'll be fine."

He took her in his arms.

"I'll be back before you know it."

She nodded, then dropped her head onto his chest as he hugged her tight.

"Goodbye, dearest."

His heart leapt as she used her pet-name for him, once more.

"I love you, Polka."

He held her hand for a moment, then made himself turn and

leave. Presto handed him his mask and tank, and before long the two friends were astride Scales and heading for Cadence Falls!

***

As Scales brought Landler and Presto down to land, a scene of near-chaos met their eyes, for there was quite a heavy Cascade in progress.

No one had seen them land, for all eyes were on the Waterfall and the cascading Dots, so it came as quite a shock to Fling and Stem as they returned from the Warehouse to see Landler and Presto!

"Is it bad?" asked Landler, waving away the Gnome's greeting.

"Not *so* bad, Landler. We'd be fine; it's just that we're short-handed."

Landler looked round and saw that at least half the Gnomes were missing.

"Where are they, Stem?" Landler asked, worriedly. If people were already ill…

"In the gardens - gatherin' in all the food."

"Woodwind's comin', they say!" added Fling, scratching his head, as if he didn't quite believe it, himself.

"It *is* lads. That's why…" he broke off as a particularly large flurry of Dots escaped the Fairies and Gnomes and headed off to the Bar Barrier.

Souza, flying above, (though *much* farther back than Landler had done!) shouted "Swarm!" but before anyone could follow it, Scales was off flying after it, masks, tanks and all!

He stopped short ahead of the swarm, turned and flanked… not *at* the Dots, but across their path so that they were forced to turn back in the direction of the Falls, where they were safely gathered up and taken to the Warehouse.

A great cheer went up as folks realised, not only that help had arrived, but Landler and Presto had returned, too!

Forlana turned, frowning, but then caught sight of her brother and flashed him a quick smile and a wave, which he returned, before carrying on with her duties.

From overhead came, "Come on now, no slacking. Back to work!" Souza's expression changed as he suddenly saw his leader, but Landler gave him a mock salute to indicate he should continue in the role.

Presto surged forward with the others, as yet more Dots appeared at the top of the Falls and, after a quick glance round, Landler decided they had it all well in hand, so he set off down the little alley that led to the Gnomes back gardens.

He'd just reached the first one when he stopped short and stared in amazement!

For there, in the gardens, helping the Gnomes and working as hard as any of them, were the two Goblins who'd kidnapped Polka! He couldn't believe his eyes, but Polka had been right; they <u>didn't</u> go running back to Dee Sharp the second they were free!

Sackbut called across to the next little garden.

"Lilt! Are these gooseberries ripe enough to pick?"

"Should be!" Lilt called back. "Pick 'em anyhow; no sense leavin' 'em for the mist to spoil!"

Sackbut turned back to the bushes and began to pick with a will.

Landler walked up to the following gardens and tapped the nearest Gnome on the shoulder.

"Right! Where can I help?"

"Landler!" Glee clapped him on the arm. "Can you go and dig up some taters in Shawm's garden? That takes the longest… Mist comin' soon?"

Landler nodded and, grabbing a shovel, spent the next hour harvesting whatever could be used. Eventually, they all loaded up barrows with the produce and trundled them round to the Warehouse.

Seeing that the Gnomes had the storage of them well in hand, Landler went back to the Falls to see if he could help there, but he found the clear-up operation was almost over.

All at once, a figure came hurtling towards him and Landler held out his arms to hug his sister.

"Landler! Thank goodness!" She looked up at him, as if checking he was alright. She must have been satisfied, for her next words were: "Where's Polka?"

"Oh yes, Polka. Well… er… she's needed at the Red Barn… distilling, you know."

Forlana had enough on her plate, without worrying her with his concerns about Polka, too!

But Forlana, who knew Viola very well, frowned at him.

"I'd have thought Viola could have managed…"

She was interrupted by Presto who, with his jaunty stride, came over to ask a question.

"Hi, Forlana. I've just been told that the Fairies who got caught out in the Woodwind are in the Treatment Centre?"

Forlana gave Landler an apologetic look.

"Um… yes… about that…"

Landler grinned at her.

"You used my old home?"

"Well, you see… we needed somewhere…"

"It's a brilliant idea!" he said, squeezing her arm. "Why did you think I'd be angry?"

"Well, you've only just moved out! But the Maestro thought…"

"He was right, of course; I don't need it anymore, after all."

His expression suddenly changed.

"But who's sick? What happened?"

"We've been so lucky, Landler! There's been no wind for a day or so, but Roundel and Mallika went beyond the Pizzicato Pool to gather some more herbs, when suddenly the Woodwind was blown right up behind them, before they had time to run! They managed to get back alright, but now they're both ill."

Landler and Presto exchanged worried glances.

"We've brought masks and oxy-tanks. Once the Woodwind arrives, everyone must wear one if they need to go outside. Presto will show everyone how to use them."

"Good." Forlana linked arms with both of them, as they walked slowly back to the Warehouse.

"Where are we going?" asked Presto, mystified.

"Some things have had to change in preparation," Forlana replied. "The Warehouse is now our centre of operations: everyone gathers here for the evening meal and, when the Woodwind does arrive, it'll be where we all stay until it's passed."

Landler nodded.

"The Maestro's idea?"

"Dash and Crumhorns, actually. And that reminds me, Landler, about the two Goblins…"

"I know," replied her brother. "I couldn't believe it when I saw them working alongside the Gnomes, earlier!"

"They've worked as hard as everyone to get all this ready; Dash and Lilt have done wonders with them!"

She suddenly remembered the other piece of news she must share with them.

When she had finished, Landler looked sceptical.

"Lee Van Clef's long-lost brother? That doesn't seem very likely, sis! Are you sure?"

"Not me, the Maestro!" replied Forlana. "After all, we were only younglings when Dale disappeared; I don't even remember what he looked like!"

"Presto?" Landler looked at his friend.

"If the Maestro thinks it's him...?"

"I suppose so... Well, Lee will be the only one to confirm it... <u>when</u> we can get him here!"

They got some food, and were just sitting down to a nice, hot meal when Catch, who was on look-out duty, called out:

"Woodwind! It's coming!"

Forlana was on her feet in a second.

"Right! You all know what to do! Catch, you and Glee get that cover in place, over the chimney! Ocarina! Bank the fire down. Klang, organise a team to secure all the windows! Presto! Bring Scales inside - he'll have to sleep in here!"

She'd shouted at him, before she'd realised he was right next to her. He grinned and ran off to do her bidding.

Soon, everything was ready. Scales had been made comfortable in the far corner; Landler, after asking Forlana what <u>he</u> could do, was sent to make an overall check. The fire was banked now, so that only the thinnest plume of smoke rose up to the clever contraption that Glock had made, which would let the smoke <u>out</u>, but nothing could get <u>in</u>!

Forlana glanced around at the pale, worried faces of her friends and called out, "Minima! How about a song?"

Minima caught her meaning at once and went over to the small platform where the Gnomes were already tuning up. She spoke to them, and soon a rousing, merry song filled the air, with everyone joining in the chorus.

Forlana quietly returned to the table, having first asked Fretta to check on their patient and reassure him.

Landler took Forlana's hand and patted it.

"Well done, sis."

CHAPTER 21

The following morning, it took everyone a few seconds, upon waking, to remember that they weren't in their own homes anymore; they were, in fact, altogether in the Warehouse, with the evil Woodwind surrounding them outside!

A couple of younglings started to cry and so Minima, after a nod from Forlana, went over to sit them all down and tell stories to calm them.

Glee and Bell had covered the night-watch and went to report that, although not too dense, the Woodwind was, indeed, all around them now!

"I must go!" cried Landler, springing up.

"Not before breakfast." Forlana pushed him towards the tables. "Scales has to eat too, remember?"

Landler scowled, but after a hearty breakfast he had to admit he felt a lot better.

He turned to Presto. "Right, you know how to demonstrate the oxy-tanks?"

"Landler… I <u>made</u> a lot of them!"

"Sorry, of course you did. I just don't want any accidents…"

"I'll make sure they all understand, I promise!"

Landler smiled wearily at his friend.

"I'll leave it all in your capable hands, then."

He rose and went to find Forlana.

"Scales and I have both eaten, so <u>please</u> may we leave now?" he asked, teasingly.

"I suppose so… just don't get yourself killed."

"I won't," he promised, giving her a quick hug.

After checking that Scales had ingested enough Flame Rock, Landler was about to put on his mask, when Scales added, "That's nearly the last of it though, Landler. I wasn't counting on doing so much flaming on this trip!"

"That's alright. We can go back to the Crescendo Range, if need be, as soon as we return to Scores Hall."

"I've got another sack in my quarters, as well as these," the little dragon said.

"Good. We'll fill 'em all!"

With that, Landler put on his mask, switched the button on his oxy-tank to 'ON' and climbed aboard.

The Gnomes swung the big double doors open just enough for the dragon to get through, while several Fairies stood with huge leaf-fans, ready to wave out any mist that tried to get in.

As it happened, Scales' first massive down-sweep of his wings cleared it all out, anyway and the doors were quickly closed.

The Journey to Scores Hall was the most difficult one Scales had done, so far.

Although the gathering mist wasn't yet heavy, it constantly swirled around them, obscuring their vision.

In fact, it was only when Scales flamed a section away that the little dragon could see where he was going!

But, when they eventually reached the Hall, Landler realised how lightly Cadence Falls had got it, for Scores Hall lay muffled under a thick green blanket of mist!

The Woodwind had settled, and looked as though it had no intentions of leaving.

Fighting back a sense of panic, Landler applied pressure with his left knee, and Scales altered his direction, slightly, searing a large patch of mist as he went… then they both saw the top of the tower looming up right in front of them, and Scales veered smartly to the right, taking them past it and down to the near grounds outside his quarters.

'Idiot!' thought Landler, 'why did I try to make him change course? he knew where we were - I didn't!'

But he didn't have time to dwell on it, as Scales landed abruptly, just in front of the large doors. He lifted a heavy foreleg and banged hard.

A tiny slit appeared between the doors, then Landler could hear voices shouting. As the doors were dragged slowly open, Scales helped by pushing from his side, (knocking several Fairies backwards in the process) but it made the whole thing quicker for, as soon as he was in, the little dragon turned and pushed the doors shut again, sweeping the Woodwind with his wings as he did so!

Landler quickly climbed down, removing his mask and tank.

A huge cheer went up, as people saw who it was!

Fanfare hurried towards him.

"Landler! So good to see you! Is Scales alright? We have so many sick Fairies and creatures here, that I'm not sure how we'll cope."

He looked at Landler with tears in his eyes.

Landler immediately thought of Brand, but he had much to do now, before he could go back and check on Polka and his Beamer friend.

"Don't worry, Fanfare - we'll manage," he said, with far more assurance than he felt. "Could you find the Maestro for me, please?"

"Oh of course, at once!"

Fanfare sped off, with only one more glance in Scale's direction.

Landler smiled at one of the Fairies.

"Timp, could I ask you to organise some food and water for Scales? He's had a long flight, and I know Fanfare won't be easy until he's taken care of."

Timp, the retired Professor who had been teaching Scales to play the drums, smiled.

"I've been wandering around here, wondering how I could make myself useful ever since we were all brought inside! Glad to have something to do!"

"Thank you, Professor!" Landler laughed.

He turned to Scales. "Go and have a good meal and a rest, now; you did a wonderful job getting us here!"

"Thank you, Landler!" Scales was delighted by the praise; he turned to follow Timp.

"... and Scales..."

"Yes, Landler?"

"I'm sorry I steered you wrong at the tower. I should have trusted your instincts."

The little dragon bowed, then went after his Professor.

Just then, a tread he knew only too well came hurrying down the tunnel that led from the main building.

"Landler!" The Maestro came and grasped his shoulders in welcome. "It's good to see you! We are managing here, just."

"I've brought masks and oxytanks, Maestro, so that your people can fetch more supplies, if needed."

He called three of the Fairies over, gave a quick, but exact demonstration of out to use both mask and tank, then left them in charge of storing all the equipment, (which strong hands had removed from Scales as soon as he'd entered) and going round the various groups of Fairies throughout the hall, making certain that they, too, knew what to do.

That done, Landler then accompanied his master to the study where, hung on the wall, a huge, embossed copy of the Circle of Fifths hung. Monody reached up and pushed the letters which named each key, in a certain sequence - C,G,D,A,E.

"Call Great Dragons At Eventide," murmured Monody as he pressed each letter. "That's how I remember the sequence," he chuckled quietly.

As he pressed the gold circle, the door to the secret chamber opened.

Landler glanced briefly at that circle. It seemed to him that, maybe, something was missing from the middle of it. There was a circular-shaped hole, right in the centre, which looked as though it ought to contain something else.

Landler had meant to ask the Maestro about it the first time he'd seen it, but with all that was happening <u>now</u>, it wasn't the right time.

He followed Monody into the chamber and sat down, waiting for the others to arrive but, to his surprise the Maestro shut the chamber door and took his seat.

"Maestro?"

"I wanted to talk to <u>you</u> first," said Monody, seriously.

Landler took a deep breath, then put all his anxiety and fear into his next question.

"What are we going to do, Maestro? How can we possibly survive this?"

The Maestro looked steadily at his second, then placed the tips of his fingers together.

"I <u>think</u> there <u>may</u> be a way," he began, slowly, "but it's never been done before, so I don't know if it will work."

A tiny glimmer of hope began to surge in Landler's heart.
He looked with pleading eyes at his master.
"What do you plan to do, Maestro?"
"Monody took a deep breath.

"Bring <u>all</u> of them… all at once!"

CHAPTER 22

Rollo came into the main barn, rubbing his eyes. Now that the mad dash to make the masks and oxy-tanks was over, all he really wanted to do next was sleep for a week!

However, Rollo knew that, now Landler had gone, he must pick up all the threads of leadership again that he had gladly given to Landler whilst they were all so busy... He saw Polka sitting alone, so he went over to her.

"Morning, Polka; may I join you?"

"Of course." She looked up at him with such sadness in her eyes that Rollo was alarmed.

How could Polka have changed so much in just a few, short days?

Her face, once plump and merry, was now pale and drawn; she'd lost a lot of weight and Rollo saw, with concern, that she'd been crying.

"Polka," Rollo took her hand. "Whatever is the matter?"

Polka looked at him, hopelessly.

"He's gone, Rollo; he doesn't love me anymore - I don't think he _ever_ really wanted to be with me."

Rollo stared at her in horror. Polka, who always had a sunny smile and a kind word for everyone. Polka, who forgave the two Goblins who kidnapped her! Polka, who loved everybody as much as they loved her!

With tears in his eyes, Rollo beckoned Viola over.

"Take her to the sickbay," he whispered, "I thought we'd got to them in time at Pavane Villa, but now..." He spread his hands, sorrowfully.

Between them, they got Polka (who was now sobbing desperately) to her feet.

"We need Landler back!" said Viola, worriedly.

"I know!" replied Rollo. "But how on Octavia are we going to let him know?"

If anything happened to Polka, Landler would never forgive himself!

***

Landler, meanwhile, was busy trying to convince the rest of the Circle that Monody's plan would work (even though he wasn't entirely convinced himself!)
"<u>All</u> of them?" shrieked Professor Cloche, "And where, may I ask, are you going to put them?"
The Maestro looked at each one in turn.
"Here," he said simply.
Even Landler blinked, looking at his master in amazement, but he quickly schooled his features and nodded.
"And <u>then</u> what?" cried Cloche, jumping to his feet.
"Professor Cloche!" Madame Leider's rich voice rang out. "You forget yourself!"
The short, stout professor looked at the assembled group, flushed and sat back down.
"I'm sorry, Maestro," he began more quietly, "I really am, but I can't see a way out of this." He slumped in his chair.
"I'm not saying I have the answer to <u>everything</u>," said Monody, gently, "but I do believe <u>this</u> plan gives us the best possible change."

There was silence around the table, whilst everyone pondered on this new information.
Fanfare, who had been invited to remain; (for even though Landler was <u>there</u>, he would have to leave again soon, so Monody felt his aide may as well be kept in the loop) coughed gently and, from his stance beside the Maestro's chair, said quietly, "Transportation?"
Monody smiled.
"Yes, that's <u>another</u> problem that needs addressing. I shall give it some thought." He looked round the table at all the worried faces turned towards him.
"If you will excuse me, I shall go and see what may be achieved. We cannot afford to wait!" He rose, bowed once and was swiftly gone.

The remaining five fairies all looked at each other in silence for a moment, then everyone began talking at once.

After a few seconds, Landler raised his voice.

"Please! We're not going to solve anything all talking over each other like this!"

Everyone quietened down, but not before Professor Cloche said, testily, "And what is he going to do if this grand plan of his doesn't work - somebody tell me that!"

Both Fanfare and Landler drew breath to reply, but before they could say anything, voices could be heard in the outer chamber. Landler quickly put a finger to his lips for silence.

"Well, he must still be here, because Scales is here!…" Then the study door slammed.

Landler rose.

"They're looking for me - sounds urgent."

This had the effect of breaking up the Circle as Fanfare went to check the coast was clear before letting Landler leave the 'study', then the others came out, one by one.

Landler set off towards the main hall, but a Fairy waylaid him just as he turned the corner.

"Landler, quick - to the quarters!"

He wasted no time running in the direction of the tunnels that led to the Magical Creatures Quarters, but what he saw made him rock back on his heels, for there, spread-eagled on the floor, his colours muddy and grey, lay Brand!

He raised pain-filled eyes to Landler's and thought one word at him… "POLKA!"

CHAPTER 23

"Not again," muttered Peri, "My fingers ache!"

She and Faye had been practising their new duet again and again, but now they really needed a rest. Faye's mum had brought a tray in for them, so they sat and had a snack.

"Going back to what we were saying earlier," began Peri, "do you think this 'Greenbow' is ever going to turn up?"

"I don't know," Faye replied, slowly. "He hasn't, so far, and nobody <u>ever</u> tells us anything about him, other than they wish he was there. It's very mysterious!"

"I wonder what he did that was so special?" asked Peri.

"He <u>must</u> have been good at playing something," replied Faye. "After all, <u>that's</u> what the Music Fairies keep telling us; they need - good musicians!"

"Yes, but <u>why</u>?" argued Peri. "<u>All</u> of the Music Fairies are good musicians of one sort or another, so why do <u>we</u> have to be?"

"Well… because the Inspiration Sprites have to come into our world to inspire composers, so… our music must be as important as theirs!"

"Ooh - that's clever," Peri said, admiringly. "I hadn't thought of it like that."

"It's just what <u>I</u> think," Faye smiled, "I'm not saying it's <u>right</u>… just an idea."

"Well, it's a good one… but it doesn't get us any nearer to getting back there!"

"Come on, Peri," Faye pleaded. "We said we weren't going to waste time going over and over it. There's <u>nothing</u> we can do, so let's just talk about something else… what do you think Greenbow looks like?"

"Um…" Peri thought for a moment, "I bet he's like some sort of Robin Hood, in green tights with a green bow and arrow!"

Faye burst out laughing.

"What good would a bow and arrow be to the Music Fairies?"

Peri chuckled and shrugged.

"I think," Faye went on, "that he's probably a really good violinist." She waited for Peri to grasp her meaning.

"Oh… of course!" laughed Peri, "A violin <u>bow</u>! <u>I</u> should have thought of that!" She touched her Clef Crystal, which was set in a tiny violin. "But violin bows aren't green!"

"Well, maybe his was," replied Faye.

Both girls began to laugh, but were stopped suddenly as, without warning, sparks suddenly shot out of their Clef Crystals.

There was no Sparkle Path in sight, so they only just had time to grab each other's hands, before they were lifted off the ground, flung hard against the far wall and then… disappeared through it!

SNEAK PEAK OF BOOK 6

"Tutti"

CHAPTER 1

Landler sat grimly astride Scales, silently willing the little dragon to go faster, even while knowing he mustn't tax him.

The Maestro, summoned from his study by the news that a Beamer had crash-landed outside the Quarters, looked drawn and exhausted, but Tanto, told to fetch his master with all speed, failed to notice.

"Please will you come, Maestro. It's Landler's Beamer, Brand; he looks to be in a terrible state! ... And Polka's very ill!"

Monody, lurching from one crisis to another, felt in a pretty terrible state himself, but Tanto would not have guessed it from the calm reply.

"Of course, Tanto. Thank you for letting me know."

Message delivered, Tanto left to see what other errands may need doing.

Once he'd arrived at the Quarters, it hadn't taken the Maestro more than a few seconds to assess the situation, for, after projecting that one thought of Polka crying, engulfed in sadness to Landler, Brand had collapsed, unconscious.

Landler had rushed to his friend in horror, and by the time Monody arrived on the scene, he looked every bit drained as his master felt!

"He's still breathing!"

"Good."

Landler turned in anguish. "Maestro, do you know about the infusion?"

Fanfare broke in. "Flame berries and nectar? Yes... Forlana told me. I'll look after him, Landler, don't worry."

Fanfare dashed out to get some Fairies to start making it immediately, while Landler looked round for Scales.

The little dragon had, in fact, heard the crash outside the doors, and, alerting the Fairies, had helped open them and drag Brand inside.

He'd then gone back to close the huge, heavy doors, and was now busy fanning the remaining wisps of mist out of the air vent.

"Landler," the Maestro began, in his gentlest voice, "I'm afraid you can't…"

But at this point, Scales had come over to them.

"Scales! Polka's sick - I <u>have</u> to go!"

"Of course, Landler."

"Just a moment!" The stern voice of the Composition Magician halted them both in their tracks.

Monody looked at Landler's pleading face, then at Scales' curious expression and sighed. He ought to forbid the pair of them to go <u>anywhere</u>, but he was wise enough to know that, in <u>this</u> instance, arguing would be futile.

Shaking his head slightly, he gave in.

"Go find your mask and tank, Landler."

The tall Fairy rushed to fetch it.

"Scales," Monody looked him in the eye. "You <u>cannot</u> rush to get him there! If we lose <u>you</u>, we lose it all - do you understand?"

The little dragon looked serious and nodded.

"You'll stay at the Red Barn for at least two days… AT LEAST! You'll eat and you'll rest… PROMISE ME!"

"I promise," replied Scales in a small voice because the Maestro sounded almost angry with him.

As if reading his thoughts, the Maestro made himself relax and smile, as he patted the little dragon.

"I'm not cross <u>with</u> you… I'm worried <u>for</u> you; can you see the difference?"

"Yes, Maestro," he nodded, much happier now. "I see, but I want to help Polka, and <u>she</u> needs Landler."

"Yes she does. Now, have you chewed enough Flame Rock?"

"Yes, Maestro. But the bag I left in my Quarters is nearly empty now, too!"

"Don't worry," Monody smiled a secret smile, "I know where I can get more!"

Landler ran back in and skidded to a halt in front of his master.

"GO!" Monody gripped his arm in farewell. "Look after Polka; we'll look after Brand."

Landler took a long look at the Beamer, then looked back to the Maestro and nodded, grimly.

He clambered up onto Scales' back.

The heavy doors were heaved open, Scales helping where he could, and after one crouched spring the little dragon disappeared into the mist.

The doors having been closed once more, Monody turned his attention to Brand. They had no Beamer <u>Medics</u> at Scores Hall, for the butterflies seldom became ill, but there were, of course, Beamers working in the rooms that Faye and Peri had visited on their stay at the Hall, so, as Fanfare returned, Monody said, "Sorry to send you off on another errand, my friend, but do you think it would be a good idea to get Brindisi down here? She can communicate with Brand in ways we cannot."

"Yes, yes, of course. I'll fetch her." And he was off again.

Monody felt the need to sit down for five minutes. The day had barely begun and he'd already had a meeting with the Circle to tell them of his idea, then implementing that idea had very nearly drained him of <u>all</u> his powers, and <u>now</u>, he sat watching a magical creature whom he'd admired and respected, hovering on the brink of death, because he had been desperate enough to try the impossible so he could tell his best friend how sorely he was needed.

How many more sacrifices would have to be made before they could end this malice and evil once and for all?

Had the Maestro but known it, Landler, now well into his journey with Scales flying steadily, was thinking exactly the same thing!

Printed in Great Britain
by Amazon